CROSSFIRE AT BROKEN SPOKE

CROSSFIRE AT BROKEN SPOKE

•

Terrell L. Bowers

AVALON BOOKS

THOMAS BOUREGY AND COMPANY, INC.
401 LAFAYETTE STREET
NEW YORK, NEW YORK 10003

PRINTED IN THE UNITED STATES OF AMERICA
ON ACID-FREE PAPER
BY HADDON CRAFTSMEN, BLOOMSBURG, PENNSYLVANIA

With love, for my mother, Lajetta Bowers Hansen, who was my role model in learning self-reliance and tenacity.

Chapter One

Luke Mallory saw the man sitting atop his horse at the crest of the hill. He recognized John Fairbourn from the adjacent ranch. He was sitting like a statue, staring out across the open fields toward the Hytower place. Luke had a pretty good idea what was going on in the man's head.

At his approach, John became aware of him and turned in the saddle. A smile of greeting came into his face as Luke pulled up next to him.

"Beautiful day," Luke offered. "Nary a cloud in the sky, wind is calm, not too hot. I could stand a few more days like this—about three hundred and sixty-five a year."

"What brings you out here, Mallory?"

"Looking for that sister of yours. We've got to finish designing our house. With four rooms, it's going to take some planning."

"Be as big as our place. A lot of space for only two people."

1

"Once we're married, I don't think we can trust to luck that it will stay at two for very long."

John shook his head. "I have a hard time thinking of Timony as a wife and mother. She's been my little sister for so long, I still consider her a kid."

"I'm facing an equally scary notion, becoming a husband and then a father one day." When John did not respond to the comment, he continued. "I expect it won't be as hard for you to step into the father routine. Timony has told me how you about raised her and Billy, after your folks passed away."

"Tough responsibility, raising kids."

Luke peered out over the open range. It was too far to see the next ranch house, but he knew who lived there. "You contemplating visiting the Hytowers?"

John sat back in the saddle and heaved a sigh. "It ain't proper just yet."

"You can visit Mont without anyone saying anything. The man is your neighbor."

"Not a single soul would believe I was going to visit Mont. He's a nice old boy, but there would be no doubt I was only trying to call on Cassie."

Luke understood. Cassie was as pretty as a bouquet of flowers, but she had only been a widow for a couple weeks. There had been no love in the marriage, but that didn't alter formal wedding vows.

"There are some unusual circumstances here, John," Luke pointed out, after a few moments of silence. "Way I heard it, Cassie was pretty much forced into marrying Preston, Plus, even before he was killed, the pompous swine paid big money to push through a divorce. Any man who treats a woman like he did Cassie, I'd say she shouldn't be expected to mourn his loss."

"Protocol, Mallory, protocol. I can't start courting her

so soon. She has to be able to hold her head up in town, look the gossips in the eye, that sort of thing.''

"You could always do it on the sly."

John shook his head and sighed mightily. ''I'm not made that way. I have to be patient.''

"Patience isn't always easy, and sometimes not even smart. You recall how Timony about scalded my hide for making her wait for me. I thought I had a good excuse too, learning the lesson that I wasn't cut out to be a Wells Fargo agent. Reckon you remember how she didn't see it that way.''

"I do seem to recollect you were in hot water for a spell.''

"How does Cassie feel about this waiting game?''

"She knows it is a necessity. Both of us agree the wait will be worth the effort, but it sure don't make it any easier.''

Luke sat for a time without speaking, both men involved with their own thoughts. Luke was able to plan his future, uncertain as his livelihood was. In a very short time, he would be a married man, responsible for a wife and home. It was a totally new concept, having someone else rely on him, expecting him to be there each night, someone with whom to stand side by side and face life's challenges. He had been a loner all of his life. It was going to take some getting used to.

On the opposite side, he could think of nothing more rewarding than coming home after a hard day's work to find the woman who loved him waiting at the door. He felt there was a great strength in the unity of a man and a woman being together. He hadn't been a part of a family as a kid, but he knew it was the way it was meant to be.

"So where can I find your sister?"

John returned to the present with a jolt, as if he had

forgotten Luke was even at his side. He showed a sheepish grin. "Off in a world by myself there for a minute, Mallory. Why didn't you hit me with something?"

"I've been that way myself a lot lately."

"You'll find Timony over at the eastern pastures. She took grub out to Token and a couple of the boys about noon. I doubt if she'll make it back to the house much before dark."

"I'll mosey over that way and see if I can find her."

John neck-reined his horse around. "I'll go with you. I'm not doing a whole lot of good sitting here like a coyote staring at the moon."

"Glad to have the company."

"Such as it is," John replied. "I'm sure Timony will tell you that I haven't been much company as of late."

"A woman can do that to a man."

"Yeah, tell me about it."

Some hundred miles away from Broken Spoke, an iron cage on wheels was rolling across a stretch of wasteland, headed for the Territorial Prison outside of Rawlings. It was a hot and dusty ride in the back of the closed-in wagon, surrounded by steel bars and an iron gate. Quanto sat in silence, his mind working as he absently listened to the other two convicts swap lies with one another. The three of them were on their way to prison, where he personally had been sentenced to twenty years of hard labor.

Quanto had not yet resigned himself to being incarcerated for the next two decades. Facing long odds was something he had done most of his life. Born to an Arapaho mother and buffalo-hunting father, he had never fit into either the Indian or white society. Toughened from birth by living out in the open, skilled as a hunter and tracker by the time he was ten, he had grown up pretty much without any friends. Until he met Yarrow, he had never laughed, never drunk, never gambled, and had never been with a woman.

For a moment, he thought back to the often-smiling gunman. Yarrow was a man who could smell a dollar or a fight. He always knew the side to choose so as to come out on top. At least, he had until he took the job in Broken Spoke. Even then, if it had not been for the arrival of John Fairbourn and Luke Mallory, they would have gotten away clean. Quanto suffered a moment of sorrow. From their first job together, Yarrow had treated him like a regular guy, never a half-breed Indian. They had formed a friendship, a bond of trust and understanding between the two of them. Yarrow had shared equally with him, their food, their winnings, even the occasional wild night in town. There was no name calling and no one had made fun of Quanto when Yarrow had been around. A killer, a gun for hire? Maybe, but he had been Quanto's first real friend.

Now he was dead. It didn't matter that it had been Tito Pacheco, Luke Mallory's Mexican pal, who killed Yarrow. Quanto put the blame on John Fairbourn and Mallory. Tito had entered the picture much like a hired gun, brought into the fight only because of his friendship with Mallory. Quanto didn't hold it against Tito for being quicker on the draw than Yarrow. Even his dead partner would have allowed that Tito had earned the kill. It was the way of Yarrow's reasoning.

As for his own actions, he had no regret over having killed Preston Hytower. The man deserved a bullet. The real mistake was Yarrow's infatuation with Preston's wife, Cassandra Hytower. Chasing after her had caused the delay that thwarted their escape. It had been a fatal procrastination for Yarrow and resulted in Quanto being convicted of murder and sentenced to twenty years in prison.

He quietly brooded over the hands of fate while he planned for a chance to get even, to have his revenge against Fairbourn and Mallory. The ideas were fertile in his mind, and he had the skill to carry out his plan. As he considered the options, he knew he was going to need help. It caused him to consider the two other prisoners.

Cracker was a thin man with a long face, who had the habit of endlessly cracking his knuckles. He bragged of having broken into and robbed over a hundred stores in twenty-five different towns over the last five years. Only the waking of a protective dog had caused him to get caught. Several of his previous crimes came to light at his trial, so he was convicted of theft and robbery and shipped off to prison.

Lariquette was half French. He had a bit of an accent, but it seemed more for show than anything else. He claimed his grandfather had been with the Hudson's Bay Company, one of the fur traders, who helped map more than a million square miles of Canada between Lake Superior and the Pacific Ocean. According to him, it had been his grandfather, not David Thompson, the man who was given credit for the undertaking, who actually traced the Columbia, the Mississippi, and the Saskatchewan Rivers. If it wasn't enough to make up stories about his grandfather, he also professed that his own father had been a noted guide for the Handcart Company, the one responsible for leading thousands of Mormons to their Zion in the Great Salt Lake Valley in Utah. If that was the case, none of the religious dedication of those people had swayed his own path. A card sharp by trade, Lariquette's only claim to fame was having killed another man during a card game in Pine Bluff, after he had been accused of cheating.

''Tell you what I'm going to miss the most,'' Lariquette announced. ''It's the mademoiselles, the pretty ladies. I have nothing but fond memories and dreams to help me survive the next four years.''

"For me it's the drinking," Cracker complained. "Daggone it! Two years without so much as a beer. I'll be crawling up the walls at night!"

"How about you, my friend?" Lariquette asked Quanto. "What is it that you will miss most?"

Quanto paused to take note of the terrain. They were miles from the nearest town, without a farm or ranch in sight. He rotated his head around and put his flinty eyes on the Frenchman. "I'm not going to miss anything."

"Nothing?" Cracker was shocked by his statement. "You mean, you won't miss drinking, or chasing women, or fishing, or hunting, or even taking a ride across country—nothing?"

Quanto's lips pulled back to bare his teeth. Not a sneer, but not a smile either. "I won't miss those things, because I'm not going to prison."

Both men exchanged looks.

With a glance to make certain the driver was occupied with directing the team and the outrider guard was too far away to look into the back window, Quanto sank down onto his knees and strenuously began to work on the heel of his boot. He turned his foot sideways and twisted and pulled at the heel until it came off. Tucked into the heel was a small, odd-shaped key.

"What do you have there?" Lariquette asked.

"A friend of mine named Yarrow was smart enough to make me carry one of these at all times. He had a fear of being arrested."

"Say now, mister." Cracker was instantly friendly. "Whatever you've got in mind, I'd wager it would go smoother with three of us working together."

"Can you open the locks to our shackles?" Lariquette wanted to know.

Quanto did not reply, but stuck the end of the key into the wrist iron lock and began to work it around. The lock gave way and he had one hand free. "Progress is a wonderful thing," he said with a sneer. "I remember when they used to hammer rivets to secure the wrist and leg irons on prisoners. Might as well give us invitations to escape, locking us up like this."

Cracker laughed. "If you're going to get out of here, I'm sure ready to make a break with you. No way I want to spend the next couple years behind bars."

"Nor I," Lariquette agreed. "What is our plan?"

Quanto finished removing his chains. "They'll let us out for the noon meal and some exercise in a couple hours. The idea is to keep the shackles in place long enough to catch them off guard. We jump them, grab their guns and throw them into their own cell and lock them in. Then we drive the wagon off the main trail and take the horses to escape. Someone will come along and find the guards in a day or two."

"And then what?" Cracker wanted to know. "We're going to need money and mounts, saddles, tack, supplies—can't get far on one horse and the wagon team."

"I know the place to get us some all the money we'll ever need. There's an old guy over at Broken Spoke who inherited himself a whole herd of cattle coming up from Texas. Before I was transported to Cheyenne for trial, I heard he was going to ship the lot of them back east to the slaughterhouses. That means a pile of money, probably fifty thousand dollars or more."

Cracker whistled at the news.

"Count me in too!" Lariquette was equally enthusiastic.

"Then let's get ready. We'll only have one chance at this."

Chapter Two

Timony Fairbourn was exhausted from the long hours of standing. She and Sally Kensington met up with John at the general store. He was finishing with the loading of a few supplies. Rather than offering to help, she climbed up and sat down on the wagon seat. She arched her back to relieve the stiffness. Sally followed after her, sitting down at her side. John joined them a few minutes later.

"So how did it go?" he asked as he picked up the reins and took off the brake.

"Do you know why marriage is supposed to be forever?" Timony said wearily.

"Commitment, love, fidelity?"

"No, it's because no woman would ever want to go through the infernal nuisance of having a second wedding dress made!" She gave her head a shake. "I swear, John, when this is over, I might never wear white again. I'm getting real sympathetic to those scarecrows you see in the farmers' cornfields. No one or no thing should have to remain in the same position all day long.''

John smiled at Sally. "I'd say my little sister must have had to do a lot of standing."

Sally giggled. "Like a statue for two hours."

"Seemed a whole lot longer to me," Timony said. "Sally and Mrs. Devine must have used a thousand pins to hold every fold, hem, and seam. Not once, but a dozen times over. I swear, you'd think they were having me act as a model so she could sew this outfit for the Queen of England."

"It's going to be beautiful," Sally said. "I hope, when I get married, Mrs. Devine will help me with my dress." She dug into the pocket of her dress and removed an immaculate white handkerchief. "This is what I'm going to have my wedding gown made out of, it's pure silk!"

Timony reached over and rubbed it between the tips of her fingers. "That would be like wearing a shroud of leaf silver, Sally. It would take a dozen underskirts to keep it from clinging to you like a second skin."

"And that's a bad thing?" she asked, laughing.

Timony stared at the lace-edged piece of cloth. "Who monogrammed your name for you?"

"Mama did it. It was a birthday present for when I turned sixteen. I've had it for almost two years now—I take it with me everywhere I go."

John started the team moving and glanced at Tom Kensington's eldest daughter. "I've heard of a few guys trying to court you, Sally. Have you got yourself a steady fellow yet?"

"I'm still looking over the offers," she said smugly. "There's plenty of guys around, but not many who would make good husbands. I'm not going to choose the first bull I run across, not until I have time to look over the herd."

He chuckled. "You sound like you were raised on a ranch, rather than a farmer's daughter."

She showed a wide grin that displayed a couple uneven teeth. Rather than detracting from her smile, it seemed to add character. "I'm not a bit prejudiced about whether it's a cow tender, railroad man, or farm boy, John. When the right one comes along, I'll be ready to snag him."

"I saw you at the dance last month," Timony put in. "I don't think there was an eligible man or boy in the valley that you didn't turn an ankle with."

"Yep," she admitted, tucking away the silk hankie, "I'm going to take a taste of every flavor before I decide which is my favorite. A girl only gets one chance to say yes to the right man."

The trail back to their ranch ran adjacent to the Kensington farm. John turned the wagon down the lane to drop off Sally at her house. They saw Tom off in the field as they passed. He waved from the distance, but continued his work. Once they reached the yard, John and Timony exchanged farewells with Sally. She hopped down and he headed the team back up the dusty lane toward the Rocking Chair Ranch.

"That girl has become a hopeless flirt," he observed, after a short distance.

"She is something of a tease," Timony agreed. "There's been more than one fight started over her around town."

"I suppose she'll grow out of it one of these days, once she finds the guy she's looking for."

"She had better learn to watch her step too. When she baited Billy into dancing with her at Cartwell's last month, I thought Leta Cline was going to pull her hair out."

"Might be the start of a war all over again."

"Imagine that, a couple of farmer girls fighting over one

of the cattlemen,'' Timony said. ''Have things changed in this valley.''

''You're right, kid. It's sure been a lot more peaceful with the farmers and ranchers all getting along. It's only been a few months since Tom would have taken a gun to us for crossing onto his land, and here his daughter is helping with your gown.''

''The barbed wire was a blessing in disguise,'' Timony agreed. ''Our cattle still have run of the range, but the crops don't get trampled underfoot.''

''Not to mention, it brought Luke Mallory into our midst.''

Timony smiled. ''Thanks, John. My aching body needed a reminder as to why I'm so stiff from standing.''

''If you love him, he must be worth the effort.''

''For a time today, I was beginning to wonder. Sally and Mrs. Devine could not seem to make up their minds about the design, the flounce, the hem, not anything about the dress. I swear, I about told them both to forget it.''

''Can't fault them for wanting it to be perfect. After all, they probably never made a wedding dress for anyone as pretty as you.''

Timony cast a sidelong glance at her brother. ''I don't think you've ever called me pretty before.'' At his shrug, she smiled. ''Must be the influence of a certain young lady in the valley.''

John was not the most communicative man in the world. While Timony and Billy were always teasing and passing gossip back and forth, John was reserved, several years older than both of them. He had long since taken on the job of being head of the family. It had separated him from much of the idle chitchat and ribbing that was normal between brothers and sisters. Only on a rare occasion had he opened up to her. She felt this was one of those moments.

"I can't think of anything but her, Timony," he confessed. "Mallory told me that was normal. He seemed to be doing some daydreaming about you."

"I'm glad you told me," she replied. "I'd hate to think that I'm going through all of this torture while he was being nonchalant about our relationship."

"I wonder if Billy will ever get this way?"

She laughed. "Leta Cline certainly hopes so. I spoke to her at the dance, before Sally talked him into a dance and about started a war. Leta was doing the usual complaining about him. She worries that he takes their association too lightly. She is ready, even eager, for their relationship to progress into more than a once-in-a-while courting."

"He's a very young twenty-three, much less mature than I was at that age." John sighed. "I suppose I'm to blame there. I never gave him much responsibility. I've always let him do pretty much as he pleased."

"I think he's growing up, but not at the speed Leta wants."

"Haven't seen much of Billy for the past few days. Seems that fellow of yours is keeping both of you busy."

"Billy and Cully Deeks offered to help with the windmill. Mrs. Devine said Bunion had been out there too. During a dry spell, it would be a blessing for everyone around, if there was a place to get water."

"I agree."

"Besides, if Luke had tried to build the thing all by himself, he would never get started on our house. I told him I wasn't going to live in a tent. The shanty on his property is not much more than an Indian hut. I won't set up housekeeping in a one-room sod hovel."

"You could have brought him to live at the ranch. I've told you before that you're welcome to live there with us."

"Sure, have two brothers watching every move we make—how romantic."

John was silent for a few minutes. When he spoke again, he was staring straight ahead, as if he didn't have the nerve to watch her expression.

"How long do you think I should wait, Timony?"

"Before you start courting Cassie?"

"Yeah."

"She was made a widow when Preston was killed," Timony reasoned. "As he had pushed through a hasty divorce decree, some might consider her to be a divorcée instead. Around polite society, I suppose either case would mean a wait of at least a year."

"A year?"

"But," she hurried on, "Wyoming is a hard and untamed country. We aren't even a state yet. I should think half that would be plenty."

"Christmas then?"

"That ought to be reasonable for a formal courtship to begin. Until then, sitting together at church or going over to visit her and Mont would be unacceptable behavior."

"Even for those like Linda?"

Timony recalled how their foreman's wife had reacted to John's interest in Cassie, before she was free of her marriage. Piousness knew no rank or order in their society. What the woman felt was proper behavior from a Christian point of view was something that could not be argued.

"She will come to accept whatever you choose, John. You can't please everyone in the world, you can only live with your own decisions. Once she gets to know Cassie better, I'm sure she will construe your actions as acceptable."

"I want you to know that there wasn't anything between us," he said, making eye contact with her. "I mean before, while Preston was still alive. She offered her hand to me one time and I held it for a second or two, that's all. No inappropriate words passed between us, there was nothing like that.''

''You don't have to tell me what I already know, John.'' She gave him a reassuring smile. ''I've always been proud of what a righteous man you are, as good and honest as anyone I've ever known.''

He seemed to relax. ''I appreciate your support and suggestions about this, Timony.''

''Both Billy and I will be behind you, whatever you decide. If the two of you want to start seeing each other officially, we will understand.''

''Like I said, you're going to be one beautiful bride.''

''Flattery isn't going to sway my opinions, but''—she smiled a second time—''it surely can't hurt.''

Edna Ingersol stood before the Kansas City mayor and town marshal, awaiting the release of her children. She despised their conceited airs, the lift of the two men's chins. They were like all of the other hypocrites in town, full of their own pomposity and importance.

''You must promise not to return to this vicinity, Mrs. Ingersol,'' the mayor articulated, as puffed up as a river frog laden with his fill of night flies. ''The judge would not go easy on your kids a second time.''

''I done told you, my brother and his two sons was done kilt back a spell,'' she explained for the second time. ''Me and the kids are rightful heirs to their farm.''

''And you claim the property is over in Wyoming Territory?''

''Place called Broken Spoke.''

''Amber and Donald still owe another fifteen days on

their sentence," he reminded her. "If I release them, I'll expect you to leave the city forthwith."

She hooked a thumb over her shoulder at the wagon and her two other sons. "Leland and Ray have the wagon loaded. I ain't aiming to do nothing but put this burg of popinjays behind me."

The judge gave a nod of his head and the marshal went into the jail to get the two Ingersols. While waiting, the judge cleared his throat and displayed a look of concern.

"I wish you the best of luck, Mrs. Ingersol. Perhaps having a farm to work, your kids will have less time on their hands for mischief."

"They ain't no never-mind of yourn, Judge. They's all good kids."

"Poisoning Widow Lane's dog with wolfsbane and hanging it over her doorstep is not an acceptable prank. She dearly loved that dog."

"She shouldn't a gone bad-mouthing Amber like she done at the church social," Edna countered. "She had it coming."

"Amber showed up wearing Levi's, Mrs. Ingersol. The Bible clearly states that a woman shall not wear the clothes of a man, nor a man the clothes of a woman. The Widow Lane is a very righteous Christian."

"Didn't give her the right to call my Amber a sinner," Edna snapped. "Lucky for her that my kids only strung up her dog. Had Barney still been alive, it might have been the old hag herself."

The judge locked his jaw, as if to hold back a string of harsh words. The marshal saved him any further exchange, as he returned with Amber and Don. The two hurried over to stand next to Edna.

"Good to see you, Ma," Don greeted her.

Edna's hand moved swiftly and she slapped him smartly

across the cheek. Before Amber could step away, she slapped her too.

Amber gingerly rubbed the side of her face with one hand and pointed at her brother with the other. "He was the one who done it, Ma. I only got grabbed 'cause I was with him at the house."

"It was 'cause of you that Donny got in trouble!" the matriarch of the family hissed. She gave a tilt of her head toward the waiting wagon and the two of them hurried to join their brothers. Edna gave one last look at the two authority figures.

"We'll be leaving now."

"Good luck," the marshal said. "I hope you do real good in Broken Spoke."

The judge also added his blessing. "Yes, our best wishes for a safe journey."

"You kin both drop dead," Edna retorted acidly.

"That's telling 'um, Ma," Ray gloated from the driver's seat.

She spun about and walked smartly over to the wagon. Don had remained on the ground, there to help her find the steps for climbing aboard. Once she was seated, he got into the back with Leland and Amber. Ray took off the brake and put the team into motion.

The judge and marshal watched the Ingersol family head up the street. Once they disappeared at the far end of town, they both uttered a sigh of relief.

"I don't envy the folks of Broken Spoke," the marshal said. "Those kids are about as manageable as a family of wolverines."

"I spoke to one of the Wells Fargo teamsters about Miller Queen and his sons, the three who were killed a few weeks back. From the way he talked, those boys were not much better. Can you imagine owning up to having Edna and Miller as your offspring?''

''Their mother should have stuffed them both into a sack at birth and tossed it into the river.''

''We can be thankful for one thing, they are no longer our problem.''

The marshal spat into the dust at their feet. ''Amen to that, Judge.''

Chapter Three

Luke Mallory stood back and admired the week's handiwork. It was the fifth day of working on the project, but the Halladay Standard windmill was finished. Set high enough to be in the almost constant wind and breezes, with the shaft driven down to the water table belowground, it was likely to produce two or three hundred gallons of water per day. The water storage tank would collect all that was needed for the house, while the second line from the well pipe would terminate at the watering trough for the animals. With a pump handle at the junction, he could control where the water went, or simply shut it off when it wasn't needed.

"Just the way the Halladay Standard looked in the farm journal," the youthful Billy Fairbourn remarked, removing his gloves. "Soon as Cully ties in the pump shaft, you're in business."

Bunion joined them, scratching at his shaggy beard and

squinting skyward, trying to see how Cully was doing, working atop the tall structure.

"Can't hardly see Deeks, he's up there so high. You sure he's still there?"

"Completing the final tie-in," Billy said. "We've about got this baby done."

"Being up that high would make an old-timer like me dizzy," Bunion remarked again. "Good thing there's you young roosters to do the climbing about."

"I sure couldn't have done it without all of you fellows lending a hand," Luke said.

"If you'd have built your house over next to the creek, we could have saved all this work. It would have been no trouble to run us a gravity trough or pipe from the stream."

"Wasn't a level spot for half a mile down that way. Besides which, the gnats and mosquitoes seem to flock to the water in the late evenings. I've always wanted a porch where I could sit and watch the sunset."

"Starting to sound like a married man already."

"I appreciate your help, Billy."

The young man grinned. "You think with my sis chomping at the bit to walk the isle with you, that I had any choice?"

"Once I'm done covering the roof of the house, it will be ready to finish inside."

Bunion looked over at the half-built construction. "Nice of Mont Hytower to send over enough material to do the foundation and walls. It's lucky for you that he decided to have a smaller house built for himself. Probably even gave you a good price on the brick."

"I still owe him for it. Don't know where I'll get the money to pay him."

"You could go back to doing teamster work for Wells Fargo," he suggested.

"I checked with the branch office, but they didn't need any help."

"Well, something will come up. At least Mont isn't the type to hound you over a few dollars for materials. After selling off that big herd of Texas longhorns and leasing out his Hereford bulls, the one thing he doesn't have to worry about is money."

Billy removed his hat and fanned his face. It was unusually humid for Wyoming weather, even in the month of August. There were a few scattered clouds, but they were quickly moving across the sky with no sign of rain. Luke took a drink from his canteen and offered it to the youngster. He held it for a moment, before putting it to his lips.

"John's been a bear lately. When do you think it would be okay for him to start courting Mont's niece?"

"I spoke to him about it the other day. He seems eager enough, but is reluctant because of tradition and moral standards."

"Yeah, there's some gossip around town about her, being that she's a new widow and all. He doesn't want to mar her reputation."

"I suppose there are always going to be those who meddle in other people's affairs. As for myself, I never really figured it out—is Cassie a widow or a divorcée?"

Billy shrugged his shoulders. "A little of both, I expect. The divorce was pushed through a couple days before Preston was killed. I suppose her last name isn't really Hytower now."

"Mont took her in, same as if she was a widow and still related to him by marriage. If he is willing to make that sort of commitment, I'd say he has passed judgment for the rest of the valley. That's good enough for me."

"Yeah, John too."

"But?"

"Well, there's folks like our foreman's wife, you know, the ones who like to talk. They think John ought to stay his distance for a year or so, I guess to show suitable respect or mourning.''

"Hard to mourn a tyrant like Preston. He came into the valley and tried to take it over. He abused Cassie, treated her like dirt, even gave her to a killer as payment for working for him. I don't see behavior like that justifying any code of ethics, only condemnation.''

Bunion wandered over to offer his opinion. "Can't pay no never-mind to the squawking of a few hens. If John loves the gal, he ought to haul her before Cartwell Devine, say the vows, and the devil to anyone what don't like it.''

Luke gave his head a shake. "The lady has to live here. She probably prefers to be a part of the polite society in our fair valley, Bunion. Can't blame her for wanting to be accepted, rather than being an outcast.''

"Yeah,'' Billy agreed, "women need to hold their heads up, be a part of church or social doings, have a say in domestic stuff and all.''

"Domestic stuff.'' Bunion snorted his contempt. "One day, the women will have us leaving our guns at home, slicking back our hair like some fancy groomed cat, shaving the beard from our faces every day, and even taking a bath every week.''

"You think a bath is a bad thing?'' Billy asked. Then he poked his elbow into Luke's ribs. "That explains a few things, eh?''

"Yeah?'' Bunion took the bait. "And what would that be?''

"Oh, you know, why you get along with horses so well, why skunks sit up and take notice when you ride by, and how come there ain't no flowers growing around the livery.''

"You've a real sense of humor there, sonny."

"Just don't ever go to sleep out in the open." Billy continued to joke with him. "A couple of hungry vultures are liable to come along and confuse your scent with that of a rotting corpse. They might try and eat you alive."

"You young whippersnapper, I've a mind to have me a talk with John. I'm commencing to think he never whupped you enough whilst you was growing up!"

Billy chuckled and took a swig from the canteen and handed it back to Luke. "So what about you and sis, Mallory?" he said to change the subject.

"Cartwell is going to announce our formal engagement at the Sunday meeting."

"You set a wedding date yet?"

"Not yet. Your sister has some strange ideas. She expects me to have our house built and be able to support her first." Luke moved his hand in a sweeping gesture. "I've nothing to offer but a sizable crop of rolling hills and a herd of tumbleweeds. If not for the creek running along one edge of my property, I wouldn't have a single asset."

"You've got a windmill now. That will feed a few head of stock and provide water for your house."

"Yeah, if I had any stock."

"Sis is one-third owner in the Rocking Chair Ranch and John has told her she can also have the Shire team and the large wagon. That means, even if you can't get work with Wells Fargo again, you can hire out to haul freight."

The foreman from Big George Overman's ranch, Cully Deeks, came climbing down from his perch atop the windmill. He had grease on his hands and smeared on his trousers, but a smile spread over his face.

"It's primed and ready. There's enough wind this afternoon that the blades are turning at a fair speed. Give it a try.''

Luke went to the pump control and opened it for the trough side. At first, there was a spewing of air, then a puff of dust. After a moment, a trickle of dirty brown liquid came shooting out in tiny spurts. A few seconds passed, then reasonably clear water began pouring into the watering trough. The four of them cheered and shook hands all around.

''We got company!'' Cully stopped the celebration, pointing at the approaching rider.

Billy stared at the distant form. ''Looks like Token.''

Luke wondered what the Rocking Chair foreman wanted. He was riding hard, something Token didn't do that often. He'd heard the man joke that, at fifty-plus years, he preferred to strap his saddle on a rocking chair, rather than a horse. He continued until he was in their midst, then pulled his horse to a stop and looked down at the four of them.

''Figured I'd catch all of you still here,'' he said. ''I was in picking up some supplies in town when Cole got the news in the mail. The judge in Cheyenne handed out Quanto's sentence last week.''

Bunion moved ahead a step. ''He going to hang?''

''The judge gave him twenty years in prison. There was no real proof as to whether Quanto or Yarrow was the one who did the actual shooting of Hytower. Being that Preston was linked to the death of the Queen boys and was trying to take over the valley, I suppose the judge cut him some slack.''

''At least we won't be bothered with him again. Few men live for twenty years behind bars.''

''We're finished up here,'' Luke announced. ''I've got some jerky and hard rolls, if you fellows are hungry.''

''I've got to get back,'' Cully said. ''We only figured

three days for this chore. Big George is going to be pacing the floor.''

Billy was next to reply. ''There's work waiting for me too.''

''And no telling how much business I've lost at the livery,'' Bunion added. ''I expect we all have things we ought to get back to.''

''Well, I'm thanking all of you again,'' Luke told them as a group. ''I couldn't have managed without your help.''

In a matter of minutes, Luke was standing alone, watching the subtle operation of his very own windmill. Once the house was finished, he could figure out how he was going to earn a decent living. Those were the only things between his spending his days and nights alone or having Timony Fairbourn at his side as his wife and life's companion. Thinking of her gave him an added energy. With a few hours of light yet, there was enough time to get a little more done on the house. Then he would slip down to the creek at dusk and try to catch a couple fish for supper.

Chapter Four

Cully Deeks was on his way home when he saw the
loaded wagon coming down the main road. He veered in
that direction and took note of five people on board. It
looked to be a family, comprising a young gent on the
wagon seat alongside an elderly woman, with three more
in the back, randomly scattered among a load of furniture
and belongings. The three men looked in their early twen-
ties, with a female of about the same age situated between
them. He gave her a second look, impressed by her sandy
colored hair blowing wild and untamed in the breeze. It
was unusual for a woman to expose her hair to the harsh
elements of sun and wind. The wagon stopped at his approach, but there was no greeting on any of their faces,
only suspicion.

"Howdy do, folks!" Cully addressed them with a smile.
"Where you headed?"

"What business is it of yourn?" the man on the wagon seat asked.

"Hush, Donny!" the woman scolded him. When she locked eyes with Cully, he had the feeling he had come face-to-face with a tough, seasoned she-cat. "We be the Ingersols," she offered, "blood kin to Miller Queen and his sons. Miller was my brother."

Cully removed his hat and put it over his chest. "I'm right sorry about your loss, ma'am. The Queen family were our neighbors." Biting his tongue, he added, "And friends. Their bodies were laid to rest at the town boneyard."

"And who would you be?"

"Name's Cully Deeks, ma'am. I work for Big George Overman. The Queen farm borders our south range for a piece."

"We headed the right way?"

"Yonder," he replaced his hat and pointed up the road. With a second smile, he again tried to be friendly. "Ain't more'n a day's walk for a three-legged grasshopper. You'll be able to see the fence when you top the next rise."

The woman looked off in the direction he was indicating. Cully's eyes stole back to the girl in the wagon. Surprisingly, she met his gaze, about as bold as a brass band. He might have smiled, but the three boys were staring back at him.

"What yuh lookin' at, cow tender?" one of them sneered.

Cully was careful not to take offense. "I was thinking how another gal in the valley will be a welcome addition come the monthly barn dance in town. We've got maybe ten men for every eligible woman in the valley."

"We don't socialize that much, stranger," the man chimed back.

"I'm right sorry to hear that."

"Hear what he said, Ray?" the largest man in the group said. "He's sorry."

"You two shut your yaps!" The girl hissed the words. "The guy ain't doing no harm."

"Sure, Amber," Ray said with a smirk, "we'll keep quiet. Right, Leland?"

"Ah-yeah, right." The big fellow laughed. "Like Ray says, we'll keep quiet."

The old woman waved her hand and all were silent. "We're obliged to you for directions, mister. Mayhaps we will attend one of your shindigs one day."

"Last Saturday of each month, if you've a mind to join in. They turn the saloon into a dancing palace for everyone. No gambling and no drinking, except for punch or lemonade. Just music and dancing and fun for all."

She allowed a curt nod of her head.

Cully touched the brim of his hat. "Welcome again to Broken Spoke, ma'am." He swept over the group. "Welcome to all of you." Then he put his horse into motion, an easy lope that took him quickly over the hill and out of sight.

"Guy sure had eyes for Amber," Ray observed, as soon as Don started the wagon rolling again.

"Ah-yeah," Leland said teasingly. "You think the guy was trying to flirt with Amber?"

"Appeared that way to me."

"Ray's right. The guy was flirting with Amber."

Amber kicked out at Ray, but he was too quick, moving out of her reach. He chuckled at her glowing eyes and show of temper. "You two are as blind as a couple earthworms. The cowboy was looking us all over, wondering if we was dirt."

"What do you think, Donny?" Ray asked. "Did it seem to you that he was thinking we was dirt?"

"More like he wanted to take a bite out of Amber," Don joked. "Most fellers don't want a mouthful of dirt."

"Ma!" Amber cried. "Make 'um stop!"

"That's enough," Edna said, exerting her unwavering authority. "We got to keep our minds on the problems at hand. Namely, how do we get by till next harvest?"

"I'll find work," Ray told her.

"Me too," Leland joined in. "Ain't no one can work harder than me. Right, Ray?"

"That's right," Ray said, praising him, "Leland can out-work a team of mules."

"Everyone will have to throw in to make a go of our new place," Edna said. "That means we got to be civil to our neighbors and such. Won't no one hire a troublemaker. You boys mind your manners."

"How about Amber?" Leland asked. "Don't she have to mind her manners too?"

"I mean all of you. We done got run out of the last town. That ain't going to happen again. We're here to stay. You hear me?"

"Yeah, Ma," the boys all answered as a group.

"It don't mean that I have to wear a dress all the time, do it?" Amber asked. "I mean, we 'bout come to the end of real civilization way out here. Bet no one will look twice at my wearing Levi's and a man's shirt."

"Just don't be wearing denim to the dance or Sunday meetings," Ray advised. "Leastways, not until we know that the other gals round these parts do the same."

"You don't know what it's like to be stuffed into a heavy bodice, a thick material skirt and a couple of horse-blanket petticoats. You ought to try wearing twenty pounds of dry goods and see how it feels."

"Price you got to pay, Amber," Don joked, "if you want to draw the attention of the young bucks around town. It sure seemed that you were getting your share of attention from that stranger."

"I ain't looking to get hitched to no man's wagon, Donny!"

"You're old enough for sparkin' under the moonlight," he replied. "Don't tell me you ain't never thought about it none."

"I seen her reading one of those romantic-type penny dreadfuls one time," Ray said and snickered. "I'll bet she's looking for one of them there white knights, one what comes along and saves the damsel in distress."

Leland laughed. "Ah-yeah, Ray, she's looking for a white knight."

"There you are, Amber," Donny continued to razz her, "you only got to figure out what a damsel is supposed to wear when she is in distress. Then your shining knight can come rescue you."

"You three are only jealous 'cause I'm the only one in the family what can read more than a few easy words!"

Edna allowed the hazing, as she knew Amber was as tough as any of her sons. When it came to sheer strength of will, she put all the boys to shame. She was a sight smarter when it came to ideas or notions, too, although that didn't keep her from getting into trouble as quick as the boys.

Pausing to consider her children, Ray was the oldest boy, but he was not a leader, unless one was to consider the way Leland followed him around. Ray had always been the one to tend to Leland, and, in Leland's eyes, he could do no wrong. Leland was two years younger than Ray, but Barney had said it right one time, that the boy was about as bright as a moonless night. Edna blamed the midwife who helped deliver Leland. She had been inept. Her awkward handling of the birth had nearly killed the young boy. By the time he was delivered, he had turned blue and wasn't breathing. Only Barney blowing air into the boy's lungs, then ducking him into the watering trough had brought him around. From day one, however, he had always been slow to form an idea or do things on his own. It was fortunate that he had a patient and caring brother like Ray to look after him.

That left Donny, who was fifteen months younger than Amber's twenty years, her baby. He was quick, smart, with the qualities of a man, but he was a prankster and often got into trouble. Without asking for details, she knew it had been his idea to get even with the widow Lane by killing her dog. Amber could be hard as nails, but she had a fondness for animals. She wouldn't have gone along with harming the widow's dog. Donny was the opposite shoe. He had always enjoyed hunting and killing. If there came any real trouble, he was the one she would put in charge.

Turning back to Amber again, she didn't consider her a striking beauty, but she didn't have the long faces of the boys. When she put her mind to it, she could be comely. Swift of wit, with an impish smile and seductive, smoke-colored eyes, and enough hair to stuff a mattress, she had attracted a few male admirers over the years. To this point in her life, however, she had never done any real courting. Edna blamed a share of that on her three rowdy brothers, but Amber also had a way of putting men off. She wanted to be in control of any relationship and do things her own way. She had a flash-fire temper and was not above using her fists like a man. Edna compared a number of girls in Amber's position as the only girl in a house full of boys. It seemed they either grew up as tomboys or they were totally pampered by overprotective brothers. Amber was the former.

The wagon topped the crest of the hill and rolled past a barbed-wire fence. Edna looked off into the distance and was able to see the top of the house. It was located in a natural cup of sorts, with gently rolling hills to three sides. The crops had gone to mostly weeds, but the fences were standing straight and tall, still firmly in place. That would keep the wandering cattle from coming onto their farm. There was a cavity off a short way, where water had collected to form a pond, but it had gone dry. With the creek running a course at the bottom of the hill, it looked feasible to route a little of the water to the lower field for watering. They would be able to dry-farm on the hillside and raise whatever they could down near the creek. It was a good place, a farm of their own.

"Is this it, Ma?" Donny asked.

"This be home," Edna replied. "We're through moving around from town to town. Broken Spoke is where we are setting down roots."

"Yuh think there's any fish in the creek?" Leland asked no one in particular. "Bet there is," he answered his own question. "Yup, I'll just bet there is. First thing, once we get the chores done, I want to go fishing."

"We'll need a little money to see us through, Ma," Ray said. "We don't have but a few dollars in the family fund."

"Soon as we get settled, you boys can start looking around for work. We'll get by like we always done."

"Yeah, Ma. We'll make out just fine."

"Not much of a house," Don said. "Mostly sod, except for the rock chimney."

"Looks pretty small from here," Ray observed. "One corral and no outbuildings at all. Bet there ain't but one room in the house."

Edna remained resolved. "We'll make do. It's home."

Chapter Five

Cassandra Granger ran the brush through her hair and stared at the face in the mirror. It seemed like a lifetime ago that she had been married to Preston. She was thankful for Mont, Preston's uncle, who had taken her in like his own niece. Although Preston had pushed through a hasty divorce, Mont still recognized her as a Hytower.

Pausing in thought, she recalled the cruel, quick-tempered man to whom she had been married. He had forced her into matrimony to save her mother's life. The sacrifice had been for naught, as the woman had been too sick to survive. After her death, Preston had forced Cassie to study ten hours a day, bringing in tutors to teach her how to talk, how to walk, how to maintain a social posture, how to dress. He had tried to make her into a live doll, someone totally subservient and disposed to his every whim and demand. Moving to the edge of civilization, Preston

had sought power and might, attempting to become a cattle
baron and king of the territory.

Burdened with cooking and the household chores, Cassie
had not been able to live up to his idea of a queen. Preston
had become verbally and physically abusive, until finally
cracking under the strain of his empire. Except for the un-
spoken promise she had seen in John Fairbourn's gaze,
Cassie had hated her existence.

Her focus returned to the blond hair and rich chocolate
eyes in the looking glass. She could smile again, free of
the tyrant who bartered her to a gunman named Yarrow.
She had been payment for the hired killer. Both Yarrow
and Preston were dead. She was owner of her destiny once
more, filled with optimism and hope for the future, her and
John's future.

"You about ready to go?" Mont's voice came through
her door. "Fairbourn will be over with his carriage any
time. We don't want to be late for the Sunday meeting."

"By the time he arrives, Uncle, I'll be ready."

"All right. I'm going to . . ." He stopped in midsentence, and there was the sound of the front door opening.
Cassie listened, but her uncle and someone were suddenly
speaking in hushed tones. She felt a rush of anticipation,
certain it was John. Her heart rate increased, she experienced a mild giddiness, and she took a moment to make a
final inspection in the mirror. Every hair was in place, her
touch of rouge just enough to highlight her naturally
healthy complexion. It was time to go.

"Hey! what's—?"

Mont's words were cut short, and there was another
noise—it sounded like a body falling against the table! She
hurried over and opened her door. She glimpsed Mont lying
on the floor, a split second before something dark and black
swooped down over her head. Hands grabbed her and she

swung blindly at the aggressor with her fists. She made
contact and a man cursed. Backing away, she tried to reach
up and remove the bag, which was about to smother her.

Too quickly, strong arms wrapped about her and pinned
her hands. While prevented from defending herself, a second assailant took hold of her wrists. Terror turned her
heart to ice and robbed her of her breath. She struggled
against the two attackers, but it was futile. Her hands were
jerked around behind her and a cord was tightly bound
around her wrists. Within seconds, the sack was secured
with a string around her throat.

''Don't give us a reason to hurt you,'' a growling voice
hissed. ''You be good, you live. Cause us any trouble and
we'll skin you alive!''

Cassie halted the futile resistance against her captors.
''What about Uncle Mont?'' she whispered through the
sack over her head. ''Is he all right? Did you hurt him?''

''Shut up!'' a second voice snarled, ''or I'll plant a fist
in that pretty face of yours!''

Rough hands guided her out of the house. She was lifted
up onto the back of a horse and a rope was wrapped about
her waist. From the feel, she knew they had tied her to the
saddle horn, so she wouldn't fall off. Then, as fear shredded
her very soul, her horse was being led away at a rapid pace.

With Timony at his side, Luke felt about as proud as the
only bull in the herd. He was dressed in his best suit of
clothes and had polished his boots till a man could have
used them for shaving mirrors. He felt the envious looks
from several of the eligible men, as well as the approving
looks from the women in town.

Timony had donned a fashionable Dolly Varden dress.
It's oak brown outer skirt was attached to a matching bodice. Unbuttoned from the waist down, it revealed a lace-

trimmed, butter-colored underskirt. Rather than wearing a bonnet, her long, raven black hair was held in place with a wide, yellow ribbon.

Cartwell Devine led the prayer meeting, being that the circuit parson only visited one Sunday of each month. He paused when it came time for the local news or announcements.

"Two notes of mention today," he said, looking out over the crowd of nearly fifty people. "A special welcome to our newest residents, Mrs. Barney Ingersol and her four children." He glanced down at a piece of paper in his hand. "Ray, Leland, Don, and Amber. They have taken possession of the old Queen place. Miller was Mrs. Ingersol's brother," he explained. "And, if anyone needs some help for hire, the Ingersol kids are looking for work. Get word to me or Mrs. Ingersol and we'll set up an interview."

He put on a wide smile. "On other news, I should like to announce the engagement of Timony Fairbourn and Luke Mallory. They plan a spring wedding." There was a polite applause at the tidings and Cartwell looked at the two of them. "All of our best to you young folks."

The door opened at the rear of the room. Cartwell diverted his attention to the arrival of Timony's brother, John Fairbourn. He saw the flushed concern in his face and halted his congratulations.

"Where's Bunion?" John asked, searching the room.

"Here!" Bunion spoke up, rising to his feet. "What's the matter?"

"Mont is in the wagon outside. He's been pistol-whipped."

Luke and about everyone else in the place rose to their feet. Cartwell took over as presiding judge, rather than minister. He banged on the pulpit with his fist.

"Quiet down!" he ordered. "Let him finish. What's happened, John?"

"Two men showed up at the Hytower place and demanded Mont open his safe. When there wasn't enough money to satisfy the bandits, they took Cassandra hostage and knocked Mont senseless. They are demanding fifty thousand dollars for her safe return!"

The place was a melee, with people all crowding around John, or trying to go outside to get a look at Mont. Bunion was first out the door. Cartwell realized that he had lost control. He shouted that the meeting was over.

Once Mont was laid out in a bed and had been treated for bruises and a cut on the side of his forehead, John met with the old marshal, Jack Cole, Luke, Timony, and the mayor.

"Billy is over with Mont, in case he can tell us anything more," John began. "He came to long enough to tell me that two men forced their way into his house, both wearing masks. He gave them what money he had, but they demanded more."

"I can't believe it," Cole said, "fifty thousand dollars? Do those bandits think Mont is made out of money?"

"He sold off Preston's herd of cattle," Luke said. "Consider what he received for that and the amount he inherited when Preston died, I would guess he has access to that much money."

"Do you think they'll hurt Cassie?" Timony worried aloud. "She's a hearty girl, but still a lady. This has got to be horrible for her."

"We better come up with a plan," John said, his tight-lipped demeanor revealing his anxiety. "Men who will kidnap a woman haven't an ounce of decency in their bodies. We can't trust them to hold up their end on any kind of deal."

Luke surveyed the group. ''Who is the best tracker we have around here?''

''You're not considering going after them?'' Timony asked. ''They might kill Cassie!''

''It's a death sentence to kidnap a woman. If she can identify the men, it would make more sense for them to get rid of her, rather than turn her loose. I'm only looking for possibilities.''

John was thoughtful. ''Cully Deeks did a little scouting one time.''

''This is beyond his skills,'' Cole said. ''What we need is a specialist, someone who can track without being seen, a man who has lived by his wit and prowess all of his life.''

''You talk as if you have someone in mind.''

''An old pard of mine, Hal Everson, ran supplies during the Indian wars. He has a young Shoshone Indian who works for him. I don't know his real name, but old Hal always called him Joe. He was a scout for General Crook, back when the Army was chasing Dull Knife and the other Cheyenne from the Black Hills of Dakota to the Yellowstone Mountains. Hal said he was one of the best. Last I heard, he was breaking horses for Hal over in Rimrock.''

''Be worth a day's ride,'' John said. ''It'll take some time for Mont to get his money from the Wells Fargo office in Cheyenne.''

''Trail will be pretty cold before we can get him here,'' Luke said.

''How do we work it?'' Cole asked.

Cartwell was the one to reply. ''I think you should be the one to go fetch this Indian for us, Luke. If these here jokers know very much about Mont, they might also know that John and Cassie are on courting terms. We can't be sure if the bandits have eyes and ears in town. They might be watching John.''

"Makes sense," Cole agreed. "Those vermin also have to make arrangements for the exchange. They are going to have to contact us in some way."

"So we here, along with John, can devise a plan for dealing with that," Cartwell suggested, "while Luke brings the Indian in the back door. Once we have the tracker, we can sneak a couple men out the back way and look for the kidnappers without them being any the wiser."

"They are sure to be watching for something like that," Timony pointed out.

"We've a few new residents in Broken Spoke," Cartwell replied. "Luke can pick up a couple of the Ingersol boys to ride with them. That would give him three or four guns."

"How do we know we can trust the Ingersol family?" Timony asked. "They might be behind this whole thing."

Cartwell looked at the marshal. "I sent a wire to check on them," Cole said. "I wanted some proof that Miller Queen was actually their kin. The marshal in Kansas City wired back that he had investigated the family. They are sure enough who they claim."

"Then you don't include them as suspects?"

"Not when you figure the time needed to make the trip over here from Kansas. First off, they were all sitting in at the Sunday meeting, and second, they haven't been in town long enough to put together any scheme. I'd say we can cross their names from the list."

"Who else could be behind this?" John asked.

"Could be any of the men who used to work for Preston," Luke said. "You recall that, about the time Preston was killed, we ran a few of his hired guns out of the valley. Any one of them could have come back to rob Mont."

"So we don't have a clue," Cole said. "I guess that means we go with Cart's plan. Luke can ride to Rimrock and bring back the Indian while we figure a way to deal with the kidnappers when they contact us.''

''I'll pick up a fresh horse from Bunion,'' Luke said, agreeing to the idea. ''I should make Rimrock by midnight. With any luck, I'll be back tomorrow.''

''Sounds good,'' John said. ''Godspeed and good luck.''

Luke left the group, with Timony right on his heels. She wasn't there to stop him, only following until they could be alone. He was in a hurry, but he figured a smart man always allowed for time with his woman.

''Do you sometimes get the idea that we are never going to have a life together?'' she said when he paused to look at her.

Clasping her about the wrist with his hand, he led her into the livery. There he turned and pulled her to him. She was warm and receptive to his kiss, then stood within his arms for a short time.

''I could go to Rimrock too,'' she offered, after a lengthy silence. ''I'm as good a rider as you.''

''Better, probably,'' he admitted. ''A good portion of my riding has been from the seat of a wagon, when I was a teamster.''

''Then why not let me go with you?''

''Alone with you, out under the stars, just the two of us,'' Luke replied. ''Do you really think I could keep my mind on what I was supposed to do that way?''

She smiled. ''I'd make sure you kept your mind on business.''

He kissed her lightly on the lips. ''I'll see you tomorrow night, or as soon as I can.''

''If you sneak back into town, then you and the Indian will probably also sneak back out into the hills. I doubt if I'll see you until you track down these wretched kidnappers.''

''Then I reckon you should give me a better good-bye kiss. It'll have to hold me for several days.''

Impishly she pushed out of his grasp. ''You might need some encouragement to hurry this chore along. I'm going to make you wait.''

He groaned. ''That isn't fair.''

''Fair?'' she giggled. ''Love isn't supposed to be fair. You have to work for the rewards.''

''Yeah, right.''

''Hurry back, Luke.'' She backed up another step and coquettishly blew him a kiss. ''I'll be waiting.''

Luke watched her spin about and hurry from the livery. It was all he could do to remember the mission ahead. He swallowed the rise of passion that threatened to overrule his good sense. The first order of business was to check back with Bunion and then hit the trail. It was going to be a long sixty miles before he could rest for the night.

Chapter Six

Quanto stood at the open window and watched the sun come up. It had taken sixteen hours to make the false trails and reach the hideout. He wondered if anyone else knew of the abandoned shack. Built by hunters or trappers from years gone by, it was little more than a thatch hut, with a leaky roof and spaces in the walls wide enough to see through. The dirt floor was still hard-pack, but leaves and debris had collected in the corners of the room.

"You think this place is safe?" Cracker asked, kicking his blanket off and drawing on his boots. "I mean, I didn't see or hear so much as a coyote last night, but . . ." He let the words hang.

"It should do. We only have to get by for three or four days. I found it by accident when I used to work for Preston Hytower. It's well off of any trail or path."

"I remember, you said you used to be a hired man for the old boy we worked over."

"Not him, his nephew."

"Think anyone can track us here?"

"We rode through two cattle herds, followed the creek for a full mile and backtracked a half-dozen times. Plus, you saw me wipe the trail clean for a hundred yards three different times. There ain't but a couple men alive who could follow what little trail we left."

"I didn't know that kidnapping was going to be a part of this."

Quanto cocked his head to the side to look at the skinny man. "We didn't have much choice, what with old Mont having his money in a bank. I guessed he would have kept most of it at the ranch—I guessed wrong."

"Still, dragging that woman around, it ain't a good idea."

"You can pack your gear and ride, Cracker. No one is holding a gun to your head."

His face drained of color. "No! I didn't mean for it to sound like that. I'm in on this deal."

"So quit whining."

"I wasn't whining." Cracker quickly checked to look at the back of the cabin. "But you seen how Lariquette was looking at the woman. He sure enough has designs on taking advantage of her."

"That's why I sent him on ahead to buy the horses with the money we got from Hytower's safe. He won't be around the girl all that much."

"Until he gets back."

"He touches her, I kill him," Quanto snapped. "That ought to be simple enough, whether it's spoken in English or French."

"All I'm saying is, I don't think we should leave him alone with her, not at any time."

Quanto considered his warning. "When he returns from

buying the horses and setting up our escape, you can keep an eye on him. I have to leave to make our deal for the money and watch for any tricks.''

''I don't think he is going to be afraid of my watching him.''

''He will, if he knows I'll kill him for getting out of line. Before I leave, I'll explain it to him in words he can understand. He even touches the woman once, he ends up as a meal for the buzzards.''

''What about the gal being able to recognize us?''

''She didn't have a chance to see any of us. You had that bag over her head, before she knew we were about. Don't use no names and don't talk in front of her any more than necessary. She won't have a clue.''

''You used to work around her. Won't she know your voice?''

''I didn't say a dozen words in her presence. I doubt she recognized it was me, but it don't matter much. I've already got a death sentence hanging over my head. Twenty years in prison would be worse than hanging.''

''That's okay for you, but I was only going to serve two years. I didn't think about getting involved in something that would mean kidnapping.''

''I told you before, you can pack up and ride.''

The man began to crack the knuckles on one hand. ''No, no, I'm in this to the end,'' he said. ''I throwed in with you, same as Lariquette. I'll stick.''

''Round up some tender for the fire. With the wind blowing out to the north we should be safe enough to fix a hot meal for breakfast. I figure two or three days for Mont to get the money together. Lariquette should have everything set up for us before then. It would be nothing but bad luck for anyone to stumble onto us here, but we'll have to keep a sharp eye all the same.''

Cracker went outside and Quanto walked back to the rear of the hovel. Someone had gone to the trouble to add a lean-to against the back of the shanty. It had originally been for storing wood, saving the occupant from having to go out into the howling winter wind and snow whenever wood was needed. It made a suitable place to keep Cassandra. There was a door of sorts, a wooden partition that scraped and dragged against the hard-pack dirt floor when it was opened.

The girl rose stiffly to a sitting position on the blanket he had provided. She was awkward, for her hands were bound behind her back and a blindfold was still securely in place. It appeared that she hadn't made any effort to get loose since being stuck into the makeshift hutch the previous night. Quanto felt it was a mistake to have kidnapped her, but he wanted to make a big enough haul on this one job to never have to concern himself about money again. One thing he had decided was that no harm would come to her. Lariquette thought it would have been less trouble with her dead, but Quanto could reason that some of the people around Broken Spoke had more than muscle between their ears. They couldn't very well kill Cassandra, then have need of producing her before the ransom was paid. It was possible he would need her alive and kicking at the exchange.

''I'm quite thirsty,'' the girl said in a very soft voice. ''Could I please have a drink of water?''

Quanto about snarled at her to shut her trap, but he decided a drink wouldn't hurt. He walked out and picked up his canteen, then went back into the small lean-to. The girl moistened her lips with a quick darting of her tongue, preparing for the drink. He paused for a moment, a bit taken back at her instinctive action. Recovering at once, he put the canteen to her lips and tipped it high enough that she could drink.

After several swallows, he pulled it away. He was not used to nursing a blind woman and didn't alter the tilt of the canteen enough. As a result, he poured water down her chin and onto the top of her bodice. She gasped in surprise at getting wet, but she said nothing about it. Instead, she murmured ''Thank you'' and turned her head to use her shoulder as a napkin to wipe the dampness from her chin.

Quanto capped the canteen, then knelt down so he could get a look at the cord around her wrists. Cassandra was tied securely. In fact, upon testing the knots, he discovered a trace of blood around her wrists; her hands were cold from loss of circulation. He could tell it was painful, but she was too afraid to say anything. Again he was touched by a minuscule regret. The woman was an innocent victim. She had been responsible for Yarrow getting himself killed, but it hadn't been any fault of her own. He decided there was no reason to make her suffer.

''I'm going to untie you, but you must leave the blindfold in place. Do you hear what I'm saying?''

''Yes.''

''There's no place to run out here. You have only one chance to come out of this alive, and that is to do exactly as I tell you. Do you understand?''

''Yes,'' she answered a second time.

He mentally cursed himself for showing any weakness, but he worked the knots free and removed the cords that bound the girl. Cassandra grimaced from the effort of moving her arms. It had been twenty-four hours and the muscles were locked and tight. After a few seconds, once the circulation had returned, she began to rub the abraded flesh about her wrists.

"Thank you," she murmured again. "Being tied so tightly was really beginning to hurt."

"As I said, you keep the blindfold in place. One peek at us and you will have to be killed."

"I understand."

He stood back and looked at her. Why did he have the feeling that he was playing some silly child's game? Cassandra was no fool.

"You know who I am, don't you?" It was more a statement than a question, but he waited and watched the young woman's features. The slight darkening of her cheeks was proof of his suspicions.

She turned her head slowly from side to side. "Your voice is somewhat familiar. I . . . I'm not sure."

Quanto knew he should have stayed away from the girl, but . . . He shrugged his shoulders at the thought. "It doesn't matter. I'm already working under a death sentence."

She caught her breath. "Quanto!"

"If you give me your word that you won't try to escape, you can remove the blindfold."

Hesitantly she reached up to undo the cloth that was wrapped around her eyes. He cleared his throat. "Your word, Mrs. Hytower."

She stopped, as if he had put a gun to her head. "You trust me to keep my word, when you have kidnapped me for ransom?"

"I do."

Cassandra paused for only a moment, then nodded slightly. "All right, I give you my word, Quanto. I won't try and escape . . . from you."

He smiled at her wording of the promise. "Fair enough."

Pulling the blindfold off, Cassandra blinked at the light

that filtered into the lean-to from the next room. She lifted her head to look up at Quanto.

"How did you get out of jail?"

"Careless guards."

"I saw Mont on the floor, before someone grabbed me from behind. You didn't kill him?"

"Just dimmed his lamps a bit. I'm sure he is up and about, trying to round up a posse to come after us."

"You don't seem afraid of that idea."

"I know how to track people. It's an acquired trade. Those who have done it know what a tracker will look for. There ain't but one or two men in the country who could follow the trail we left. I have also figured it out, so when we make our escape, no one will be able to catch us." He stared hard at her. "You can be thankful for my prowess, Mrs. Hytower. Because of my careful planning, you'll be able to go free when this is over."

"I believe you mean that."

He folded his arms importantly. "The word of Quanto is as good as gold in the hand. You do as I say and you have nothing to fear."

She again gave a slight nod of her head.

"That's settled then, so let's move on. I don't like to prepare meals, and I remember sitting at the table with you on occasion. You are very good around a cookstove, so fixing meals will be one of your duties."

"What about the other men working with you? They won't want me to see their faces."

"You can do the cooking and return to your little room here." He gave the place a second look. "I'll get you another blanket."

"I would appreciate it. It was quite chilly during the night."

"Now you just sit quiet until time to cook the morning

meal.'' He placed the canteen on the floor. ''This will have to hold you until then.''

''All right,'' she said quietly. ''And Quanto?'' At his hesitation, she looked him square in the eyes. ''Thank you again.''

Quanto went out the door and closed the partition. He felt the girl was being truthful. She had better sense than to cross him. For a long moment, he stared off into space. There was something special about Cassandra, something that kindled a minute trace of compassion within him. He would have sworn such feelings were nonexistent, but they were there. He wondered why it was that some women had the power to make a man feel protective.

Thinking back, he recalled how her husband, Preston, had mistreated her. Quanto had been outside the house and overheard the man abusing her once. Learning afterward that he used his belt on her bare back, he had silently vowed to kill him. When he and Yarrow had gone to rob Preston, he hadn't cared if they got a penny from the low-life swine. He had used the opportunity to shoot him dead—and watching the man drop to the floor, he had felt good about it.

He muttered to himself, ''Durned if you ain't getting soft, Quanto. Next thing, you'll be donating money to an orphan's home or something!''

Chapter Seven

Luke stood at the corral and watched the Indian ride the bronco. He had weighted sacks strapped to either side of the animal. The horse still bucked around the pen until it was too tired to continue. At that point the young Shoshone began to teach it. There was a practiced manner about his every move, as if he knew the horse's every instinct. After fifteen to twenty minutes, he had the animal turning with the reins and stopping on command. The Indian spied Luke watching, but he didn't hurry his business. It wasn't until the horse was fully responsive to his every instruction that he brought it to a stop. The two were frozen in position for a full minute, before the Indian slipped down off of the animal's back. Crossing the corral toward Luke, he could see the man was slender, not more than five foot two or three, wearing boots, Levi's, and a cotton work shirt. His hat was a worn Army cap.

"White man want 'um talk?"

"That's right."

"What want with Tupsi-Paw?"

Luke frowned. "Hal said to call you Joe. He also told me that you speak better English than he does."

The Indian studied him for a few seconds. There was an intelligence in his eyes, plus something else—humor?

"I expect it wouldn't be hard to excel beyond Hal's limited vocabulary," he said with a slight upturn of the corners of his mouth. "The old gentleman has a tendency to murder the English language."

Luke was dumbfounded at the articulate literacy of the man. He opened his mouth, but could not think of anything to say.

"All right, I confess. My communicative skills are superior to most Indians, a good many whites too. What else do you want to know?"

"How did you manage to learn such good speech?"

"I paired off with a journalist, who accompanied General George Crook on his second Powder River expedition, back in the summer of 1876. For myself, I spent much of the time learning to speak proper English. We were together for the better part of a year and I endeavored to make a firm accounting of the language. I could speak, read, and write before my separation from the Army, shortly after the surrender of Crazy Horse."

"Why go to all the trouble?"

"Chief Washakie, of the Shoshone, said we should never fight against the white race. He proclaimed that your people had the might to exterminate the Indians from the face of the earth. As such, I deemed it important to learn all I could about the white man."

"Sizable undertaking."

"I have always had a keen eye and a good memory."

"Obviously."

"So much for my personal life history. What's on your mind, paleface?"

Luke smiled. "Name is Luke Mallory, and I'm looking for a man who can track a honeybee by the footprints left on a flower petal."

"You have lofty expectations."

"Ten dollars a week and keep."

"I don't hunt Indians anymore."

"We've got a kidnapping for ransom. We're pretty sure these guys aren't Indians."

"Ransom? Then you are hiring men for someone who has a lot of money? Is that what you're saying, paleface?"

"Name's Luke Mallory."

"Going to cost you a lot more than ten dollars a week."

"I might get them to go twenty."

"Fifty a week—a one-week minimum—and I'll bring my own horse."

"Dad gum, Joe! you don't come cheap, do you?"

"I'm as capable as anyone you can find, paleface. Better say yes, before I think about it and up the ante to twice that."

"Okay, okay." He gave in. "It's not my money. I'm in this for a friend."

"Friendship is a good thing, but not when it comes to paying for services. I'll speak to Hal and let him know I'm leaving with you. How much headstart do the kidnappers have?"

"They grabbed the girl early yesterday morning. It will be early tomorrow before we can pick up their trail."

Joe lifted his eyes to the heavens and surveyed the gathering of clouds. "A challenge then," he said.

"I reckon so." Luke looked him in the eye. "Think you can follow them?"

"If they left tracks." He grinned. "Of course, if they grew wings and flew away, it'll make it a little harder."

"You're one strange Indian."

"The word is special or talented"—he showed the grin again—"possibly even extraordinary."

"I was thinking more on the line of pompous and greedy."

"Be noon before we get started. What is it, sixty miles to Broken Spoke?"

Luke removed his pocket watch and checked the time. "Yeah, I figure we can make it by late tonight."

"I'll turn the mustang loose and saddle my horse. Meet you back at the house."

Luke said, "Right," and watched the man walk away. He was impressed by the intelligence and quickness of the Indian, not to mention his perfect English. Cole might have been smart to send for him. If he was half as good at tracking as he appeared to be at breaking horses, Joe was going to be a real asset.

John was checking on Mont's progress when Cole entered the room. He took a step, stopped, raised his cane, and pointed it at them. "Just got word over the wire, boys. I think it clears up the identity of who we are chasing."

Mont had been sitting up. He started to rise, but he was still dizzy enough that he was forced to sit back down. "What's that? Did you say you know who is behind this?"

"Wire arrived a few minutes ago from the U.S. Marshal's office," Cole reported. "Our pal Quanto escaped from the prison wagon, while it was en route to Laramie. The guards were found locked in the wagon, about half starved. You can bet a dollar against a corncob, he's behind this kidnapping."

"Quanto," John repeated the name, thinking of the dark,

swarthy gunman. ''The job of finding Mrs. Hytower just got a whole lot harder.''

''The pair he escaped with were a cardsharp gunman and a common thief. It's a good chance that one or both of them are working with him on this deal. I have the description of the two men.''

''I only saw two men,'' Mont said. ''There could have been another one outside. I didn't recognize the one who did the talking, but . . .'' He shrugged his shoulders. ''I was pretty woozy from getting clouted with the shooting end of a pistol.''

Bunion entered the room with a plate of food. ''Now, this here ain't going to work at all, boys! I sure don't intend to feed the whole lot of you.''

''Quanto escaped,'' Cole told him.

Bunion stopped, opened his mouth, then closed it. He looked at John. ''You should have killed him when you had the chance.''

''He didn't give us any reason at the time. Luke was mixing it up with him when Tito killed Yarrow. Besides, Yarrow was the gunman.''

''Yarrow might have been the fast gun, but Quanto is the man I wouldn't want to face in any kind of fight.''

''What do you think, John?'' Mont asked. ''Should I stick around the house and wait for word?''

''I don't know if they'll contact you or me—might even be Cole here.''

''How long to get the money?'' Bunion asked him.

Mont turned his attention to Cole. ''You sent word to the bank this morning. What answer did they wire you?''

''Wells Fargo is going to send the cash, but you will have to sign for it. I asked for Tito Pacheco to accompany the delivery, but he wasn't available. Seems they assigned him a new job, being some kind of surveyor. He is supposed to map out several new expansion routes for the stage. He is going to be busy for a spell.''

"He'd come if Luke asked him to," Cole said.

"Luke won't ask," John replied. "We'll have to do this alone.''

"I want you fellows to know that I intend to pay the ransom," Mont spoke again. "No amount of money is worth Cassie getting hurt. I won't risk that.''

"Our main concern is they let her go after they get the money. If she can identify her captors, they might decide to kill her, regardless if you pay the money or not.''

"So, what about this Indian Luke has gone after?''

"We're going to play it both ways, Mont," John answered. "Up front, we'll do whatever they ask. That means paying them and doing everything they tell us.''

"And meanwhile?''

"Meanwhile, Luke and the tracker will take a couple men and see if they can locate their hideout.''

"Someone mentioned he might be taking a couple of those Ingersol boys?''

"They are looking for work and appear capable in a fight.''

Bunion grunted. "What we hear, that's the only thing they are good at. Done got run out of Kansas for fighting and pranks.''

"Luke can handle them.''

"I don't know if I can sit and wait," John replied. "No telling what they are doing to poor Mrs. Hytower. She's got to be frightened to death.''

"If Quanto is involved, we aren't going to find him," Mont said solemnly. "That man moves like a ghost. He was able to shadow about anyone without them ever being aware of his presence. I remember how Preston used to assign him to someone''—he looked at John—"even you,

John. Did you know he did some checking on you? He
followed you for a couple of days once."

"I know the man is good."

"Good?" Bunion laughed. "He's the best I ever seen,
and I've been stumping across this here country for fifty
years. If he's got Mrs. Hytower, our only chance to get her
back is to do what he tells us."

"I aim to follow his instructions to the letter," Mont
said.

"So we have to wait?"

"Sorry, John," Cole answered, "but Bunion is right. We
haven't a prayer until Luke shows up with that tracker.
Seeing how it's Quanto we're after, I don't know how
much we can expect even then. Quanto is smart enough to
know what a tracker looks for. He'll not leave any kind of
readable trail, not unless it's into a trap."

John emitted a deep sigh. "I know you are right, but I
feel so completely useless. This sitting around and waiting,
it's enough to drive a man crazy."

Mont reached out and patted his arm. "Quanto never
struck me as the kind to hurt a woman, John. I'm pretty
sure he'll make us an honest exchange—Cassie for the
money."

"I hope so, Mont," John said, practically praying the
words. "I really do hope you're right."

Cully started the two strays for home. After a short way,
the two stopped to munch on a small stretch of grass near
a dry pond. He pulled up and looked toward the Queen
house. His mind automatically went to the singular meeting
with the Ingersol family. There was something about the
way the Ingersol girl locked gazes with him, as if she was
as curious about him as he was about her. Odd that it
should strike him that way. He had been around other girls

in the valley and had not experienced that kind of feeling. For a moment, he wondered if she would attend the next barn dance. He would sure go out of his way to ask her to kick up some straw with him.

Returning to the present, he checked the two cows. Their tails idly swatted at pesky flies while their heads were lowered and they grazed near a stretch of barbed-wire fence. He knew well that fence, for he had taken a beating from the Queen boys when he cut the strands that kept the cattle away from the pond. It was a much shorter distance to the pond than it was to the creek. However, there was nothing but a dry bed at this time of year. It forced him to swing around and look down toward the distant creek. He had best make sure he hadn't missed any other strays, plus his horse was probably ready for a drink too.

As he approached the creek, something white flapped in the wind and caught his attention. Upon a closer look, it was a petticoat. He stopped the horse with a yank.

"You better hold up that bronc, mister," a feminine voice warned him. "About one more step and I'll put a hole in you big enough to toss an apple through!"

Cully slowly turned his head until he could see the muzzle of a rifle. It was pointing at him as a young lady crouched behind a nearby bush. He lifted his hands enough to show that he had no intention of trying to draw his own gun.

The voice and rifle belonged to the Ingersol girl. About all he could see of her was the rifle and her wild mane of hair. Presently the long tangles were wet and laid thick against her head and onto bare white shoulders.

"You keep sighting at me thataway and I'm gonna put a socket for a third eye betwixt your other two."

Cully averted his gaze, looking straight ahead. "I wasn't intending to sneak up on you, ma'am. My horse has been begging me for a drink for the past hour or two. Because of the fences protecting the farmers' fields, this is the closest trail down to the creek.''

"If'n one of my brothers was to see you, they'd come down here and pound you into the dust.''

"Yes, ma'am.''

There was a moment of silence, as if the girl was making a decision about him. Shortly he heard the rustle of clothes. Prudence demanded that he keep his eyes forward and his hands raised.

"I suppose you're telling the truth,'' she allowed, after a few moments. "No way you could have known I was taking a bath''—a suspicion entered her voice—''lessen you was to have been watching me.''

Cully risked a sidelong glance and was relieved to see that the rifle was no longer pointed at him. In fact, the girl stood right up in plain sight. He was surprised to see that she was wearing Levi's and a man's shirt.

"I freely admit that I'd admire to look at you, ma'am, but not as a sneak in the bushes. My ma raised me to be proper respectful to womenfolks.''

She continued to regard him with a less than convinced look on her face. "I can see you don't like a woman wearing clothes like a man.''

He hesitated, searching for words that would not be taken the wrong way. At the same time, he purposely looked her over from head to foot. "How about we agree that you're not dressed in the usual garb a woman wears and let it go at that?''

"But you don't approve.''

"Clothes don't make the person, ma'am. I once knew me a cook who could whip up the prettiest salad of fresh vegetables and greens you ever seen—then he dumped a dressing on it that would gag a starving maggot. It was his own recipe and it was terrible.''

''Do that make me the dressing or the salad?''

He chuckled. ''It was one of those stories to make a point. I didn't figure to compare you to either one.''

She remained shrewd in her expression while his words sank in. After a moment, she appeared to relax. ''You told us afore that you was the foreman for Big George Overman, our neighbor to the north.'' It was not a question, but a statement. ''Him being a rancher and this here being a farm, how is it that you and my kinfolk were friends?''

''Well, to tell you the truth, we weren't all that close.'' He leaned back in the saddle. ''One time, they tried to fence off the pond up yonder. I come along and commenced to cut the wire. The two boys caught me and gave me a pretty fair whupping.''

''You lied to us then.''

''Actually, neither Miller Queen nor his boys were all that popular. They kept pretty much to themselves.'' He displayed his most winning smile. ''Reason I exaggerated was, when I saw you in the back of the wagon, I didn't want to make a bad impression.''

The smoky colored eyes remained steadfast, but the corners of the girl's mouth lifted ever so slightly. ''You trying to sweet-talk me, Mr. Deeks?''

He continued to smile. ''I'd be right gratified if I figured I knew the right words to do just that.''

''My brothers are real protective of anyone trying to get presumptive with me. You willing to risk having them trod on your hide?''

''I've an idea you're worth the risk.''

''Stop by some time and we'll see how brave you really are.''

Cully tipped his hat. ''It would be a pleasure, ma'am.''

She picked up the petticoat and several other items of clothing. Then, tucking the rifle under her arm, she started up the trail toward the house.

"Be seeing you, Mr. Deeks," she said over her shoulder.

"Yes, ma'am," he replied, "you can count on it."

Chapter Eight

Edna frowned at Ray and Leland. "You boys are about an hour late. Where you been?"

"We was fishing the creek and ran into some of the neighbors, man named Kensington. He and a couple of his kids were down filling water barrels."

"That so?"

"His farm borders ours over to the east. He has a field he wants cleared of brush and we got to discussing wages."

She perked at the news. "He going to hire you?"

"If his corn brings a good price. He and his kids could maybe do the job, but the field is more than he wants to tackle by himself. I figure with the team, Leland and I could rip out most of the sage with a chain."

"He's got himself a real purty daughter too," Leland said enthusiastically. "She done come over and was smiling at me and Ray."

Ray dug his elbow into Leland's ribs. "I didn't see her smiling at me. It was you she was giving the eye."

"Ah-yeah!" he uttered a silly laugh and bobbed his head up and down. "You think so, Ray?"

"We ain't got time for no romanticizing just yet," Edna scolded them both. "This is Wyoming Territory, boys, home of some of the hardest winters there is. We need a store of coal for the stove and staples to get us through to next harvest. If that fellow wants you two to work, you take the job."

"I'll check back with him in a few days, Ma."

"Sit yourselves down," she ordered. "Donny kilt a couple rabbits for us. They appeared to be 'bout as tough and lean as your boots, but I done stewed them over the fire for a couple hours. Should be tender enough for eating now."

Ray took a seat on one of the three stools at the table. "Think I'll scrounge some wood and make us another couple chairs. We can't even sit down together for a meal as it is."

"Good idea. Donny is off hunting coyotes. The sheep rancher, Fielding, he'll pay us ten cents for each pair of coyote ears we bring him. I guess them animals kill his lambs."

"We might all three do a little hunting then. Think there are many coyotes around?"

"Donny will know more after he gets back. If it's worth our while, you boys can go hunting too. If not, you'll have to keep asking around for work."

"Yeah, Ma."

She served up a portion of the rabbit stew to each and went back to working on a quilt. She was listening to the idle talk between the two boys when Amber came through the door. She watched her daughter dump a bundle of clothes in the corner and stand her rifle against the wall.

"After the news of that there kidnapping broke up the Sunday meeting, girl, did you even get a chance to ask around for work?"

"I spoke to a couple people, Ma. Seems there are a few Chinese in Broken Spoke. They do most of the laundry and such in town. The preacher, or mayor, or whatever he is, Mr. Devine, he said I could help in the kitchen of that Ace High Saloon a couple days a week. Guess he can use the help whenever the stage comes to town or his cook wants time off. 'Course, he won't allow me to work around the saloon part, where there is drinking and gambling going on."

"How much will he pay?"

"Four bits a day and I can keep any tips I earn from helping with the meals. He is going to give me a schedule next Sunday."

Edna studied her daughter for a moment. "I thought I seen a rider pass by, whilst you was down washing."

Amber laughed. "I 'bout put a bullet betwixt his eyes. He said he wanted to water his horse."

"Looked like that same feller who gave us the welcome to the valley."

"Yeah, Ma, it was Cully Deeks."

"He ain't all that much to look at, weatherworn from the sun, wind and all. You wouldn't get interested in a man who won't never be nothing but an ignorant cow tender?"

"He's more than a regular cowboy, Ma, he's the foreman for Big George, up the valley. I expect he could have a house of his own if he wanted. Donny says that some of them there ranch foremen make a good wage and have their own house and all."

Edna narrowed her gaze. "So you been asking about him?"

"It was only talk between Donny and me, Ma."

"You wouldn't be starting to take an interest in men?"

Amber realized that the boys had quit talking in the other room. They were listening to every word. She waved her hand, as if to dismiss such an idea. "I'd sooner have a nest of angry bees tucked into my bedding than cuddle up next to one of those mangy critters. I ain't going to bend and serve no man, Ma."

The boys laughed, but Edna continued to regard her with a thoughtful expression. "When the right one comes along, you might not feel that way. If a man loves a woman, he done treats her a whole lot better than any pack of scoundrel brothers."

"That wouldn't be much of a step up."

"I think Amber's got herself a feller," Ray suggested.

"Ah-yeah!" Leland joined in the fun. "Amber's got herself a feller!"

"You wait and see, won't be long before she'll be painting her face and brushing out her hair all purty like."

"Ah-yeah!" Leland went along with Ray, "she'll look like that Sally girl next door, all fancy and made up for courting."

"How'd you two like a fist in the snoot!" Amber shouted. "One more word about me and that cow sitter and I'll give you both a shot!"

Her anger elicited only more laughter.

"The stew is hot," Edna said, interrupting the hazing. "Pull yourself that last stool, before Leland takes a second helping and it's all gone."

"Yeah, Ma," she said.

The boys recognized the warning in Edna's voice. They refrained from any further vocal harassment. It didn't stop their smirks or their exchanging knowing looks. Amber dished up a plate of stew and sat down on the third stool at the table.

She met the silly grins with her own insolence. After a few moments, she had taken as much silent hazing as she could stand. "I recollect that Devine fellow done telling us at the Sunday meeting that Eve was the one who took the bite out of that there apple. He said it's why a woman has to suffer pain during childbirth." She pointedly looked at them both. "It sure don't seem such a sin as to explain why we have to also bear the misery of having brothers!"

Ray chuckled at her jest. Leland, as always, joined in with the laughter. He didn't always understand the joke or humor of a situation, but if Ray thought it was funny, that was enough for him.

Edna heard the approach of a horse. It didn't sound like the nag Donny was riding, so she went over and looked out the solitary window. "Company," she said.

Ray was there almost instantly to peer out into the yard. "Wa'al, don't that beat all, it's the cowboy feller what's chasing after Sis! He shore didn't waste no time."

Edna pushed the door open as the rider stepped down from his horse. Ray strode outside and, with a deliberate stance, moved to block the way of Cully Deeks.

"Howdy," Cully said, offering a smile of greeting.

"You're about as pesky as a horsefly, Deeks," Ray said. "If you've come to court my sister, you just made a long ride for nothing."

Cully showed his easy disposition again, taking no offense. "I ran into one of the fellows from town. They were headed this way to speak to you. I took the liberty of coming instead."

Edna moved out into the doorway. "Why was someone coming to see us?"

"You remember the kidnapping we learned about at the meeting yesterday?" At her nod, he continued. "We think it was some escaped prisoners who grabbed Mrs. Hytower. They are asking a big ransom for her return. We're putting together a posse to hunt them down."

"And you want my boys to ride with you?"

"Not with me, with Luke Mallory and an Indian tracker. We figure the kidnappers might be watching the town, but there's a good chance they wouldn't think about your boys joining in a special posse. It would pay two dollars a day, with a bonus if they manage to rescue Mrs. Hytower or catch any of those responsible."

"Donny is the best shot in the family," Edna said. "Ray here is pretty handy too."

"If you're interested, have your boys down at the Ace High Saloon the first thing in the morning. Mallory is supposed to be there waiting. Bunion will furnish the horses from his stable, the chuck and ammunition is being donated, so you only have to show up with your guns."

Amber poked her head out between her mother and brother. "Ain't this going to be dangerous?"

Cully paused to touch the brim of his hat in a gentlemanly gesture. "Howdy again, Miss Amber."

"That right?" Edna chimed in. "I don't want my boys getting all shot up."

"We figure either two or three kidnappers. With Mallory, your boys, and the Indian scout, they don't expect any running gun battles. If they find the hideout, they can get help in a matter of hours from any of the nearby ranches or farms. Mallory used to be a Wells Fargo teamster, so he's smart enough to not get into a major gunfight all by himself."

Edna spoke up. "My boys will be there."

"What about me?" Leland wanted to know. "I can fight just like Ray. You know I can, Ma."

"Next time," she replied in a voice that allowed no room for argument, "I need you here to tend to the chores. You hear me?"

He ducked his head. "Yeah, Ma, whatever you say."

"Besides, there are fish that need catching," she said, offering her largest son compensation. "You will have to catch a couple of our meals."

"Sure, sure, I can do that. I'm real good at fishing."

Cully started to leave, but stopped. "With any luck, this here fracas will be handled before the next monthly dance. If it is, Mrs. Ingersol, I'd admire to swing your daughter around to a tune or two at Devine's place."

"We'll see what has happened by then," she answered. "Good day to you, Mr. Deeks."

"Yes, ma'am." He tipped his hat. "Be seeing you."

Amber met his longing look with her usual stalwart gaze. He tarried a moment to smile at her, then swung aboard his horse and whirled about. As he put the horse into an easy canter, she felt the eyes of her brothers on her.

"You see him ogle little sister, Leland?" Ray asked.

"Ah-yeah." He began to laugh again. "I sure did, Ray. I sure did."

"Brothers are a curse," Amber said with a groan. "I'm going to finish eating."

Quanto met Cracker at the front of the cabin. He tipped his hat against the cold drizzle of rain. "Have to wait a minute. The girl is cooking up some grub for us."

The man shook off the water from his hands and turned up his collar. "I've been cutting wood, standing watch, and tending horses, Quanto. Now I've got to stand out here and drown while there is a warm fire and dry bed inside."

"It's only a sprinkle."

"Wet enough to catch your death."

"The lady isn't wearing a blindfold. You enter now, she'll get a good look at your face."

"So what?" He was nonchalant. "It ain't as if she is ever going to tell anyone."

"Meaning?"

Cracker bore into Quanto with a hard gaze. "Kidnapping is a hanging offense, whether in a state, territory, or even the uncharted regions of the country. Lariquette ain't going to have that woman around to point her finger at him."

"You know our plan of escape. No one could possibly stay with us. We'll be out of the country and lost forever. There's no way she can hurt us."

"Wanted posters have a habit of turning up at the most inconvenient of times. You might be willing to take that chance, but I don't think Lariquette will."

"If she doesn't get a look at you, no one will ever know you were in on this."

"We escaped together. Everyone is going to know we were in on this."

"I allowed you could cut and run before. The offer still stands."

"You're soft on the girl. I would never have expected that of you."

"I'm thinking smart. If we take only the money, the bounty hunters will eventually give up. If we kill the woman, the Rangers, U.S. Marshals, and every backyard lawman in the country will be looking for us."

"The risk still seems a lot less if we get rid of her. What she knows would die when she died."

"This is my game, Cracker. You're the one who wanted in with me. If you don't want to play by my rules, you can get on your horse and ride out."

They stood silently then, each measuring the other. Cracker shrugged. "Like I says, it ain't me. You and the Frenchman will have to sort it out. Lariquette told me the woman was going to have to be silenced forever. He's the one you have to deal with."

"It's ready!" came a call through the door.

Quanto gave Cassandra a minute to take her own plate into the lean-to. She would probably have a hard time finding a dry place, but it was certainly preferable to being bound and hand-fed by one of her captors.

He pushed open the door and made sure she had left the main room. The two men entered, shook the water off of their hats, and shrugged out of their jackets. Cracker stared hard at the closed door to the lean-to. He gave a contemptuous grunt. "She can hear our every word, and them cracks won't stop her from peeking in here to get a good description of each and all. We're sure enough going to swing for this."

Quanto glowered at him. "If you would keep your mouth shut, she wouldn't hear nothing. As for trying to see us in here"—his voice turned cold—"she knows if I see an eyeball peeking through one of those cracks, it'll get ripped out of her head by the roots!"

Cracker continued to grumble under his breath, but went over to the table and began to dish up food. After filling their plates, the two became silent with the chore of eating.

Cassie had heard the words being exchanged. She stopped chewing, her appetite suddenly lost. The sound of Quanto's voice was like the breath of death. He was capable of being totally ruthless. She had learned that he and Yarrow had calmly executed Miller Queen and his two sons, shortly before they decided to rob Preston. She was uncertain who had actually killed her husband, but John told her the bullet had come from Quanto's gun, not the smaller caliber Yarrow had been carrying.

The hunger pangs were replaced with the turmoil of fear churning within her stomach. Water dripped from a dozen cracks in the wooden slats that formed the slanted roof. There was no way to avoid all of the leaks. She had one blanket wrapped about her shoulders as she tried to force a few more bites of food.

The depression was like the dampness. It imbued her to the bone, cold and penetrating. Her world had been a topsy-turvy affair since being induced to marry Preston. His proposal had seemed the only way to save her mother's life. Instead, she had died anyway, and Cassie had surrendered her freedom to a power-hungry tyrant who wanted to mold her into an obedient doll, one who would not embarrass him when he achieved the greatness he solicited. From that low point in her life, she had innocently met and fallen in love with John Fairbourn. No words had passed between them, no illicit affair or secret meetings, it had been a distant and unproclaimed attraction. After Preston's death, she had felt that life was going to be wonderful and fulfilling. She and John could eventually begin courting and she dreamed of one day becoming Mrs. John Fairbourn.

Instead, she was a captive, a hostage being held for ransom. Quanto promised that she would be exchanged for the money, but the other two men wanted her dead. She did not doubt that Quanto was a man of his word. However, what about when he was not around? Suppose he left her with them for some reason?

She tried to put the idea out of her head. Worrying would solve nothing. She had promised Quanto that she would not try to escape. It was a promise she would keep, unless there was a very good chance of getting away clean. To be caught after or during an attempt would be to forfeit her life. Quanto would not forgive her making a fool of him.

The door scraped open and Cassie caught her breath. Quanto stood for a moment, with the light behind him, then ducked low enough to enter the small opening. He paused to look at her plate, still mostly uneaten.

"You ain't had a scrap of food since we hauled you off yesterday. Don't tell me you're not hungry?"

"I . . . I can't . . ." She struggled for any words.

"Don't pay any attention to the yapping you hear from that pup," Quanto told her, obviously seeing through her apprehension. "You and I have a deal. You keep your end, I'll keep mine."

Cassie hesitated. "I want to believe you, Mr. Quanto, but I can't stop the way I feel. I've never been kidnapped before."

"This is a business venture, nothing more. We're going to trade you for a sum of money and then get out of the country. You can go back to your life and we'll go our own way. It's simple enough."

"Perhaps if I were in your place, I would think of it as simple."

"I'll give you a few minutes more to eat. The whiner can clean up the dishes." He looked around the small hutch. "I'll get you a fish so you can keep dry."

"A fish?"

"You being from a ranch, I figured you'd know what a fish was. It's one of them yellow oilskin raincoats."

"You are very considerate."

He snorted. "That's me, a real gentleman." Then he spun about and went out, dragging the door closed once more.

Chapter Nine

"How much farther is it?" Joe broke a lengthy silence. "This rain wasn't part of the deal."

"I didn't know I was supposed to ensure we would have good weather for this hunt."

"Even a light drizzle can wash away a good share of tracks, paleface. My making this trip is probably a waste of time and effort. A couple more hours of this and the trail will be gone."

"You want to turn back?"

"I imagine it's closer to Broken Spoke than any other dry place around."

"I'd guess about another two miles," Luke told him. "We ought to be able to see the outskirts of town from one of the next rises. Saloon should still be open."

"Good. You can buy me a drink."

"They don't serve Indians at a good many saloons or

72

taverns. You know there are laws about selling whiskey to the red man.''

''The law pertains to wild Indians or renegades, my unenlightened saddle pal. Me, I'm a public servant, a domestic worker, and a sometime entrepreneur.''

''A what?''

He chuckled. ''Thought I'd get you with that one.''

''This writer who taught you the language, he some kind of professor or something?''

''He had a name, but about everyone called him scholar. That man could decorate a two-bit phrase or story with twenty-dollar words. I never saw him at a loss for a descriptive term. He was the most literate man in the outfit.''

''Well, if you get tired of breaking horses, you could probably take up writing a local newsletter or daily paper. I haven't met anyone in the past few months who handles the English language better than you.''

It was dark, but Luke felt Joe was smiling. ''How quaint, an Indian putting out a newspaper for the white masses to read. What a democratic world.''

''How'd you come to be a tracker for the Army?'' Luke asked to change the subject. ''Why help the white man fight against the Indians?''

''First off, I'm a Shoshone, a friend to the white man ever since the first one arrived in the country,'' Joe answered. ''Second, the Shoshone and the Cheyenne were enemies since long before the white men came to this land. There are stories of great battles between many factions of the two tribes since the beginning of time.''

''I didn't know.''

''The hatred runs deep, Mallory,'' Joe said, using Luke's name for the first time. ''You have probably heard of some depredations of the Indian against the whites, but it is nothing compared to the evil deeds the Indian has done against other red men. The abomination is more severe than anything you can imagine. It exceeds all decency and logic.''

''I never knew that.''

Joe sighed, as if the memory caused a great weight to fall upon his shoulders. ''You think the Indian hates the white man?'' He gave a cynical grunt. ''While scouting for General Mackenzie, we destroyed several Cheyenne camps. In one of those we found a bag of hands, the right hand of twelve Shoshone babies, gruesome trophies of some of the Cheyenne.'' His voice turned bitter and cold. ''I made a sacred oath to make those child killers pay for that.''

''And did you have your revenge?''

The man's face softened. ''We came upon Dull Knife's camp late in November, when the wind and cold were utterly brutal. During the ensuing fight and retreat of his people, eleven babies froze to death in the arms of their mothers.'' He took a deep breath and let it out slowly. ''The number was so close to being equal to the bag of hands. . . .'' His voice trailed away. After a moment, he recovered and turned toward Luke. ''I realized that we weren't fighting a civilized war. Those who were dying were not warriors, they were small, helpless children. I saw the grief of the mothers and felt the sorrow that accompanies such a loss. It destroyed my hate and will to fight.

''A few days later, Dull Knife met up with Crazy Horse. Instead of being welcomed into his camp, the two chiefs had bitter words and Dull Knife came forward to surrender. More than that, he and most of his warriors joined the white army in an effort to defeat Crazy Horse. My enemy for so many years became an ally.''

''Then, after the fighting, you left to become a free and independent man?''

''By then, I had learned the white man's philosophy, was

familiar with his beliefs and customs. When I had to choose whether I would be confined to a reservation or adopt the ways of your people, I chose to be free.''

''And the Army allowed you to do this?''

He chuckled. ''Not exactly. Hal was working for the Army during the war with the Sioux and Cheyenne. Scholar and he became good friends. I met and got to know him during those many months. When he retired a year or so back, he asked me to come along with him. My legal name is Joe Everson. Hal adopted me.''

Luke had to laugh. ''Adopted you? You must be twenty years old!''

''Closer to twenty-five,'' he admitted, ''but my adoption form states that I was sixteen at the time of signing. It was the only way to keep the Army from sending my carcass to the reservation.''

''Don't you miss your own people?''

''I think one day all people will live together in harmony, work side by side without animosity or prejudice.''

''If you're going to dream, let's eliminate hunger, greed, and disease too.''

Joe laughed. ''Right.''

''There's the lights of Broken Spoke,'' Luke said, able to spot the glimmers of lamps in the darkness. ''Sure be good to get out of this drizzle.''

''The rain is not something I bargained for, paleface.'' Joe was back to calling Luke by the epithet. ''Even the best of trackers can't follow a trail that has been washed away.''

''As you pointed out before, it seems to be mostly a drizzle, rather than a hard storm. That much is on our side, isn't it?''

''Yeah, we'll give it a try, but first you're going to buy me a couple of drinks and get me a dry place to sleep for the night.''

"I know an empty jail cell you can use. Have to share it with a mangy cat, but it's dry."

"Lead the way, paleface. I'm ready."

Timony heard the clink of a coffee cup and got out of bed. She donned her wrap and went into the kitchen. John was sitting at the table.

"It's past midnight, John. You've got to get some rest."

The redness of his eyes was proof that he had not slept in the past two days. "How can I sleep, kid?" He stared at the cup in his hand. "Every time I close my eyes, I see Cassie's face. She is probably terrified, maybe hurt—she might even be dying!" He set the cup down hard. "And what am I doing?" he vented helplessly. "I'm not doing one blessed thing to help get her back!"

"There's nothing you can do, John," Timony told him gently. "There isn't anything any of us can do at the moment."

He rolled his head back and forth. "There must be something. The woman needs my help, and we're just sitting here!"

"Do you think it would be any better out in this rain, riding around blindly on slippery roads and trails? Would it help if we got everyone in town and started to search the hills? Do you really think we'd find her?"

He simmered. "Not if Quanto took her."

"That's why Luke went to fetch that tracker, John. Quanto is a tracker himself. He'll know all of the tricks about covering his trail. I don't know if anyone can find a man like him, but we certainly can't trust to luck."

"So we are helpless to do anything!"

"Until we are contacted, all we can do is wait. Mont is going to pay the money. We are covering all bets, John. If Luke and the Indian can't find Quanto, we'll trade the ran-

som for her. Then the tracker and a posse can try and catch
Quanto after the exchange.''

John rubbed his hands together. ''It's just''—he ducked
his head—''I really hate thinking of her being out there,
being scared to death and all.''

''I know, John.''

''How about you? Don't you worry about Luke going
after a man like Quanto?''

''He's a very capable man. I have to trust his judgment.''

''That's not an answer.''

''I tend to pray a lot at night, John. It seems to help.''

''He's going to have two of those Ingersol boys with
him. I'm not sure if that increases or decreases his chances.
I don't know what to make of that family.''

''They look a little rough around the edges, but I'd say
they've been in a few scrapes.''

''More than a barber's straight razor,'' John agreed.
''Even the girl looks as tough as rawhide socks.''

''The one boy seems more like a big kid,'' Timony said.
''Leland, I think his name is.''

''He looks strong as an ox.''

''Which ones are going on the posse with Luke?''

''The other two boys, according to what Cully told
Billy.'' John shook his head. ''You know that Billy wanted
to go too. I hated to tell him that he couldn't.''

''We need him to be here, in case the kidnappers contact
us. With you spending your time over at Hytower's ranch,
someone has to be here with me.''

''He figured Token could stay with you and Linda.''

''If we're dealing with Quanto, he will know exactly
where each and every one of us are. The man is a human
shadow. He can hide and sneak around like no one else.''

''Let's hope Mallory's new scout will even the odds.

Cole said he was a Shoshone, and one of the best scouts General Crook had during the Indian wars.''

''And Quanto is half Arapaho.'' She paused. ''Haven't those two tribes been at war for hundreds of years?''

''I remember hearing the Shoshone and Arapaho were once natural enemies.''

''Then the two trackers have their own secondary war to fight, a last confrontation between two tribes who have hated one another for ages.''

''With the ultimate prize being a helpless young lady.''

Timony placed her hand on his arm and put a compassionate look on her face. ''We'll get her back, John. You have to believe that.''

He nodded his head, but there was no conviction in his features, only dread and consternation.

Chapter Ten

Bunion gave Joe the twice-over, looking him up and down. "Hardly looks Injun at all." He made his observation and stood erect. "How!" he said, raising his hand like a man swearing on a Bible, "white man greet his red brother."

Joe looked at Luke and shook his head. "Fifty dollars a day isn't going to be enough, paleface."

"Hey! He talks real good, don't he?"

"The language is English," Joe quipped haughtily. "You should take some time to learn it."

"Say now," Bunion said, objecting to the remark, "this here's one rude Injun, Mallory. I ain't altogether sure if I'm going to like him or not."

"The lad had a bad night," Luke said, excusing his attitude. "We were rained on for the last ten miles into town."

"Worse than that," Joe complained, "some moth-eaten,

79

furry critter crawled up into my face during the night and started to purr like a contented cougar. I shoved her away a dozen times, but she kept coming back. Talk about a determined, love-starved cat.''

''That would be Harlot,'' Luke informed him. ''I've spent a few nights with her before. I'm kind of hurt that she is so fickle.''

''You're sure welcome to have her back, paleface. When I got up, she began to roll around on the floor begging to be rubbed. I never saw a walking furball with such a lack of dignity, even for an animal.''

''She does thrive on attention.''

''Someone ought to tell that animal about how independent cats are supposed to be.''

Luke grinned and turned back to Jack Cole. ''So it's Quanto and a couple of other escaped convicts that we're chasing?''

''It would seem so. Here are the circulars on the two men who got away from the prison wagon with him.''

Luke took a moment to look over the piece of paper. It listed the name and description of a man named Paul Lariquette and Josh Anders, who was also known as Cracker. Joe leaned over to peer at the paper and then backed off a step.

''You want to study it?'' Luke asked him.

''I have an acute memory, paleface. That's how I was able to master English with such ease and perfection. If you like, I'll quote you the paper you're holding word for word.''

''No,'' Luke said and sighed, ''I'll take your word for it.'' Then, looking back over at Cole, he said, ''You get us some help?''

''Cully Deeks spoke to the Ingersols yesterday. Two of

the boys should be here at any time. That will give you a little firepower, should you run into the kidnappers.''

"The trail is going to be tough to follow, even for Joe here.''

"It's for sure the rain didn't help.''

"I'll pick you boys out some good horses," Bunion offered.

Joe raised a hand in protest. "If you'll pardon my disinclination, I prefer to select the animals for our posse personally. I am something of an expert.''

Bunion squinted at him from under his bushy eyebrows. "I'm commencing to think you're something of a pain too, Injun.''

"The name is Joe.''

"Your name is going to be mud, if you keep digging your spurs into me, you young whippersnapper!''

"I refuse to take credit for the fact that you're such an easy target.''

"Them there is fighting words!" Bunion howled, raising his bony fists. "Come on! Put 'um up! I'm going to whale the daylights out of you, Injun Joe!''

Luke stepped between the two of them, before the razzing got out of hand. "Let Joe pick the mounts, Bunion. What have you got for saddles? I doubt those Ingersol boys will have any gear.''

The old gent calmed down and lowered his fists. "There's a couple of old Army rigs in the barn. Ought to do the trick.''

"Let's have a look.''

Bunion paused to scowl at Joe again. "You being a scout an' all, I reckon you can find the horses all by yourself.''

"You are more perceptive than I gave you credit for, mister liveryman.''

Joe walked to the stables while Bunion stood shaking his

head. "That there is the most arrogant Injun I ever come across."

"He is smart and quick," Luke said. "If he's half as good at tracking as he is at putting the dig into someone, we might have a chance of success."

"The rain would have destroyed most of the tracks," Cole argued. "I can't see anyone finding a trail after it drizzled most of the night."

"I got the impression that Joe figured he might still find tracks."

"Then he ain't near as smart as you been thinking," Bunion remarked. "Ain't no one able to follow a trail that has been washed away."

The sound of a wagon entering town turned all of them around. Leland was driving the rig, with the two other boys sitting next to him. Each had a pistol on his hip and a rifle at his side.

Leland drove the team over to within a few feet and stopped the wagon. Once stationary, Ray and Don climbed down. Each retrieved a bedroll from the back of the wagon.

"We was told that you would supply the horses," Ray said.

"Our scout is over picking them out as we speak," Luke replied. "I'm Luke Mallory," he formally introduced himself.

"Ray Ingersol," the one replied. "This here is Donny," Then he pointed up at the large man, who had remained on the seat of the wagon. "That's Leland."

"Glad to meet you fellows. Cully tell you the deal?"

"Two dollars a day each," Ray replied.

"And you provide the chuck," Donny added.

"That's about it."

Ray turned around to face the big brute in the wagon. "Go on home now, Leland," he said, using a gentle tone of voice. "You take good care of Ma and Amber till we get back, you hear?"

"Yeah, Ray." His head bobbed up and down. "I hear you."

"No stopping to hunt or fish." He winked. "And no chasing girls."

Leland laughed. "Ah-yeah, I hear you, Ray." Then he turned the team and headed back up the street.

"He's a little slow on the draw," Ray told Luke defensively, "but that don't mean he's dumb."

"I reckon most of us operate at different speeds," Luke allowed. "I agree, it doesn't count toward a man's measure."

"So when do we start?" Donny asked.

"This way," Bunion offered. "I've got some old saddles and tack. You boys can have your pick."

"We're ready to get this here game on the road," Donny said. "Lead the way."

Luke had tracked a wounded deer on occasion, but never had he known that the job of following a trail required such a great amount of patience. From the time they left Mont's house, Joe hardly ever got onto his horse. He paced back and forth with his eyes riveted to the ground. When he would come to an indentation in the ground or find some horse leavings, he would kneel down and study them for what seemed hours.

By early afternoon, they had reached the Dakota Creek. Joe stood for a moment and looked upstream and down.

"What do you think, Joe?"

"No reason for him to lead them toward Broken Spoke. Quanto used this only as a diversionary tactic. If we miss where they got back out of the stream, it'll take us an extra day or two to pick up their trail."

"We haven't gone but about six or seven miles from the Hytower ranch house."

"This guy, Quanto, is pretty smart. They ride single file to hide their numbers, and he took us through where two herds of cattle had been recently. Now he's gone to water, so we can't track him. We have to watch both sides for any hardpan or rocky banks. He'll try to get away from the water without us seeing any markings or evidence."

"Do we have any other options?"

"If it hadn't rained, we could ride a course a hundred yards to either side of the stream, until we picked up his tracks. With the help of that storm, we could easily miss the trail."

"You really think we're going to find them?" Ray asked. "I mean, this Quanto fellow sounds about as cagey as a fox."

"He is very good," Luke admitted. "When working for Preston Hytower, he would often shadow someone for days at a time and we never knew it."

"So what's the plan now, Injun Joe?" Don asked.

"We take one side of the stream and follow it. He won't stay to water for more than two or three miles—maybe not more than a couple hundred yards. We have to spot where he left the creek."

"Which side do you think?"

"The railroad is north of here, so I would guess south. Except for the Oregon trail, there isn't a town or major outpost for a hundred miles."

"Where would they hide?" Don asked.

"A lot of natural cover out there, once you reach the hill country. They might have picked out a cave or abandoned cabin, even the remains of an Indian camp. Quanto probably had a place all picked out."

"So that's the plan?" Ray asked.

"We've no choice but to follow the creek and try to locate where they left it. Four horses have to leave prints, even if those prints will be faint after a rainstorm. We'll find their trail all right, but it might take us the rest of the day."

"Lead on," Luke ordered. "We're right behind you."

Joe started walking on foot, leading his horse. His eyes swept the ground for the slightest indentation, a disturbed rock, a crushed or broken branch, a scrape, anything that would suggest a horse had been there. As a great number of cattle often came to water along the creek, the chore was made even more difficult.

"This is going to take a long time," Ray spoke to Luke. "The breed might have kept to the water for several miles. At this speed, it might be dark before we find any trail."

"Joe is supposed to be one of the best. We'll just have to hope he can find their tracks. The delivery of the ransom gives us about two days."

"It 'pears to me, they are going to have to pay the ransom."

"My thinking too," Don agreed.

"Nothing to do but wait and see," Luke answered. "If we find where they left the creek, it might be an easier trail to follow. We could still get lucky."

"Well, we ain't going nowhere, so long as you're paying us," Ray said. "We aim to stick and see this through."

"Like Ray says," Don allowed, "we're sticking it through."

Luke watched the Indian. Each step was taken only after a careful survey. His scrutiny and patience was enough to convince Luke that he was indeed an excellent tracker. His main concern was that they were going to be too late to do any good. Once the ransom was paid, the hunt would be of a different sort. Quanto and his partners would be on the run. It would then be a chase and not merely a job of tracking. He glanced at the sun and decided their first day was not going to be all that productive. It would be dark in a few hours and that would allow the kidnappers that much more time to complete their plan.

Chapter Eleven

Amber worked hard to finish the laundry. She wanted to take a few minutes to wash her hair and maybe take a quick dip in the creek. With three brothers around the house, it was nearly impossible to have the privacy of an actual bath. As she labored to scrub the dirt from the last shirt, she looked up to see Leland coming down the path. He was whistling a mindless tune, with his fishing pole over his shoulder. When he spied her, a wide grin spread across his face.

"Gonna catch a couple fat ones for supper, little sister. Yep, you can bet I'll bring home a couple whoppers."

"Ma know you're fishing?"

"She said it was okay," he said, bobbing his head up and down. "With Ray and Donny gone, I got to put the food on the table. That's what she said."

"So where do you think the big ones are?"

"Round the bend." He pointed upstream. "Found me a

nice hole the last time I was fishing. I know there's some big ones in there.''

She smiled at him. ''If there are, I'm sure you'll catch them.''

''Ah-yeah!'' He laughed. ''You know I can. I'm real good at fishing.''

''Good luck, Leland.''

He gave a big wave and began to work his way upstream. With the scatter of brush and the occasional tree, he was soon out of sight.

Amber was glad to know where he was. It gave her a little more confidence about taking an actual bath. Not that Leland was the type to spy on her, but he was naturally curious. Being a big kid didn't stop him from wondering about the opposite sex. She recalled how Edna had once said the only girl who would marry Leland was one whose team also ran at a slow pace. Amber did not quite agree. While she didn't doubt that Leland would be an attentive and loving husband, she felt he would need a stronger force, a woman who would do the thinking for the two of them. He was an eager and hard worker, but he was not capable of planning a home or tending to a family without someone to guide him. Ray had always done his thinking for him. That was what he would need from a woman.

Satisfied that Leland was well away, Amber wrung out the last shirt and set aside the wash. She reached for the buttons on her shirt, but stopped at once, hearing the approach of a horse. Even as she stepped over to pick up her rifle, she was filled with an anxious anticipation.

She relaxed at once as Cully Deeks appeared at the clearing. Casually she lifted the rifle, pointed it at him, and said, ''You sure got a hankering to get yourself shot, Mr. Deeks.''

Cully stopped his horse, leaned back in the saddle, and

smiled at her. "Dad gum! I was hoping to catch you in the creek this time. Going to have to work on my timing."

"Are you the kind that would peek at a girl whilst she was taking a bath?"

"Oh no, ma'am," he said quickly. "I was meaning that you wouldn't have been able to get to your rifle, that's all!"

"Uh-huh."

"Really! I'm a gentleman, Miss Amber. Ain't no way I would ever take advantage of a young lady."

"What are you doing down here?"

"Came down to water my horse. I told you how it's the closest place around."

"That there's one lame excuse."

He displayed a sheepish expression and shrugged his shoulders. "Best I could think of on the spur of the moment."

"Get down off of your horse."

"Thought you'd never ask," he said, swinging a leg over the pommel and slipping down in a single motion.

Amber set down the rifle and sauntered the distance between them, her gaze locked on Cully. She could have been half blind and still read the desire in his eyes.

"Do you chase after every girl in the valley, Mr. Deeks?"

"No ma'am. I'm right choosy."

She appraised him shortly. "Why pick me?"

He showed a toothy grin. "I've a feeling you're right special, Miss Amber."

"I'm not one what swoons over a man at the first word of flattery."

"I didn't expect so."

"I'm also equal to most men on most counts."

"And a whole lot prettier too."

She studied him, wondering if his agreement was only

to win her favor. "I'm a very good shot with a rifle," she told him. "Better'n you, I'll bet."

"Could be."

"I can also outwrestle two of my three brothers."

"I would never fight with a woman"—he glanced over her attire—"not even one dressed like a man."

"You expect me to wear a hot, cumbersome dress while I'm doing laundry at the creek?"

"Only making a point, Miss Amber. I sure wouldn't ever want to fight with you."

"I figure I know what you want, Mr. Deeks," she said, swaying slowly back and forth in front of him.

"You do?"

"You want to hold me in your arms and kiss me."

Her boldness shocked Cully to his spurs. He opened his mouth, but there were no words at his command. It caused Amber to laugh at his stupor.

"What's the matter, cow tender?" she teased. "I thought you were one of those sweet talkers?"

"I never run across a woman like you before."

"You mean one who speaks her mind? One who doesn't hide behind her skirts?"

"Something like that."

"I thought you was going to come calling?"

"Yes, ma'am. The dance is next Saturday night."

"You need a special invite, do you?" She put on a coy smile. "If you had a real hankering for me, I wouldn't think you would wait for so long."

He reached for her, but she jumped back. "Not so quick, Mr. Deeks. Do you think I'm just going to fall into your arms?"

"A man can dream," he replied.

"You want to kiss me," she baited him as she turned around, "you got to catch me!"

Cully was shocked that the girl took off like she'd been shot from a catapult. He hesitated only a moment and then bolted after her.

Amber did not run like a good many girls, she was a spooked deer, a fleet-footed cross-country racer. She darted through the brush and sprinted up the trail toward the house.

Cully thought she was going home, but she turned sharply before she topped the rise to the Ingersol house. She darted across an open pasture and began to make a circle. He ran for all he was worth, but he could not even close the gap. Amber was slender and athletic, with not a hint of the knock-knees that slowed down a good many of the fair sex. She led him a hundred yards away from the trail, then angled back to the creek. Dodging and jumping brush, she reached her pile of laundry with him still a good hundred feet behind.

When she stopped, she spun to laugh at his ineptitude. "Guess you didn't want that kiss very bad!"

Cully staggered to a halt, unaccustomed to making any kind of long run on foot. He bent at the middle and gasped for air. It was an amazement to him that Amber didn't seem winded. Except for the rapid rise and fall of her chest, she showed no effects from the hard sprint.

"You're about as fast as a flushed antelope!" he said, panting.

Amber stepped over to within arm's length. "I'm faster afoot than most men."

"Is that all you do, compete with men?"

"It is, when you're raised with three brothers."

"I'm not one of your brothers, Miss Amber," he said, finally catching his breath. "I don't want to compete with you."

"Yeah, you would rather cuddle me close like a baby bunny and kiss me."

He stood up straight, for it allowed him to look down at her. He mentally deduced that size was about the only edge he had over the girl. With a narrowing of his gaze, he said, "It occurs to me that you're the one who keeps talking about kissing. I only come by to say howdy."

"Men don't want to talk to a woman, they want to gain control of her, corral her like they would a wild mustang. I ain't no horse to be haltered and broken to ride, Mr. Deeks."

"Some men want more than that from a woman."

"And what would that be?"

"A partner, a companion, someone with whom to share the pain and joy of life."

"Oh," she said and raised her eyebrows, "someone with *whom* to share. That's a real sophisticated way of saying it."

"I beg your pardon for intruding, Miss Amber," Cully said with a sigh. "I'll leave you to your washing." With that, he rotated toward his horse.

"Mr. Deeks?"

Cully revolved back around—in time to get smacked right in the mouth, with the most warm and persuasive lips he had ever imagined. Amber kissed him with such force that it about knocked him off of his feet. However, before he was able to recover enough to get into the moment, she retreated.

"That's what you came for," she told him with no emotion in her voice. "Now you can leave me alone."

Cully stared at her, dumbfounded for a moment. "Miss Amber, if that's your idea of how to discourage a man, you need someone to explain the protocol betwixt men and women."

"I told you, if you could catch me, you could kiss me," she retorted.

"I didn't catch you."

She showed a mischievous simper. "That's why *I* did the kissing."

"You are an amazing young woman, Miss Amber."

"Go on now, get on your horse and ride, Mr. Deeks. If Leland catches you bothering me, he'll pull off your arms and legs like you was a gingerbread man and it was well past suppertime."

"I still aim to come calling."

"Don't you be thinking you'll be getting another smooch," she warned. "I ain't one of those easy types. The next kiss will have to be earned, and it will have to be after we've done a bit of courting."

"Yes, ma'am."

"And don't call me ma'am. I ain't your mother."

"No ma'am."

"What?"

"I mean, I wouldn't think of you as my mother, Miss Amber. No sir! I'm for thinking I would never compare you to my mother."

She giggled at his exaggerated reply. "G'wan home, Mr. Deeks."

Cully put a foot into his stirrup and swung aboard his horse. He dawdled for a moment as he gazed down at the girl. "You're one very pretty and very exciting woman, Miss Amber."

"I expect a warning next time you come calling," she told him, careful to hide the response to his flattery. "No more sneaking down here to spy on me."

"I'll stop at the house first next time. You have my word on that."

"Good-bye."

Cully tipped his hat and forgot all about watering his horse. It was not until after a quarter-mile back up the trail before he could even get his brain to function. He put a finger to his lips, still confounded and amazed that Amber had actually kissed him. It had been a phenomenal sensation, one he intended to contemplate every night before he went to sleep.

Chapter Twelve

The sun had set when Joe sat down on the ground to eat. Beans and hard rolls were getting old real quick, but there was little more they could carry during the hunt.

"What do you think?" Luke asked, hunkered down at his side.

"It's taken me all day to be absolutely certain, but we're on the trail of three horses now, not four. When we started on the trail, there was one animal missing a shoe. That horse is not with the others now."

"What's that mean?"

"I'd venture one of the riders went in a different direction, either up the creek or back down to separate from the other three. He could have gone toward Medicine Bow, Rimrock, or Evanston—we've no way of knowing."

"Then you think something happened between the kidnappers?"

"It's possible that there was some discontent or an ar-

gument. I suspect it more likely that he will be the one to
make arrangements for the ransom, or it might be his job
to circle around and spy on the folks at Broken Spoke.
Another option would be making arrangements for their
escape. The railroad is to the south of here. They might
plan on using it to abscond once they get their money.''

''Those ideas makes sense. The kidnappers need to know
what we're up to, they have to make contact for the
exchange, and they could be thinking of using the train as
part of their escape.''

''It's all guesswork, paleface. We don't know anything
for sure.''

''Only that one of the four horses is missing.''

''That, and after twelve hours of tracking, we're twenty
miles from the creek and there is nothing in sight. Do you
have any idea where this Quanto would hole up?''

''I'm not familiar with the country in this direction. I
know there are no stage lines and no towns or settlements,
nothing but miles of empty country between here and the
Powder River country.''

''Used to be sizable buffalo herds out here on the plains,
back when I was a little kid. I remember a few hunts, before
the start of the Indian war against the whites.''

''Not many buffalo left anymore.''

''Only cattle and sheep,'' Joe agreed. ''This idea called
civilization is like a great ocean that flows to cover the land.
No power on earth can stop it or turn it back.''

''I wonder if the missing man has made contact with
Mont for the money yet.''

''Too early for that. They could not have sent for the
money until yesterday. Even if the bank or Wells Fargo has
that much cash on hand, it would still take another day or
two to arrange transport to Broken Spoke.''

''That leaves us maybe two days.''

"I took a good look from that last knoll. Couldn't see anything but a few choppy hills off to any direction."

"But we're still on the tracks of the ones with the girl?"

"I'm certain of that much. Like I said, the one horse was missing a shoe. Another has a piece of wood or something stuck into the shoe mold. Every so often, I find a print that looks to be the same horse. The last droppings we came across were about the right age, plus there aren't any other horses out this way."

"When I think of the speed of three men making an escape with a kidnapped woman, I would guess our prey took maybe four or five hours to reach this point. When you figure Quanto might have ridden all night, they could be another full day ahead of us."

"And we don't know for sure how long we have to catch up," Joe said. "The arrangements for payment might already be in the works."

"Yeah, we might find their hideout after they have already gotten their money and left the country."

"It's a possibility."

"Can we pick up the pace?"

"Not without risking losing the trail. This Quanto character is smart. He took us down two or three trails and then backtracked. Twice, I've come to a place where they have used brush to wipe the ground to erase their tracks. It's caused me a lot of time and effort to circle wide to locate the trail again. I think our quarry knew exactly how long it would take someone to pick up his trail. He probably has a plan for being gone before we can catch up to him."

"And the rain would have given him added confidence."

"Correct."

Luke did some quick thinking. "Question is, how would Quanto contact those in town about payment of the ransom?"

"I doubt anyone in Broken Spoke reads smoke, so I think we can rule that out."

"What about sending a man to contact one of the ranchers who live furthermost out? You think that might be the missing horse?"

"Possibly," Joe replied. "The third guy could have gone to a nearby town to send off the directions for the ransom."

"Or he could have contacted one of the farmers or ranchers personally."

"Who would be closest to us?"

"Big George's place."

"I recall the Wanted posters on the two men with Quanto, a cardsharp and a petty thief. If I were Quanto, I wouldn't allow either of them to make arrangements for the exchange of money for the woman. My guess would be that Quanto is the brains behind this scheme. He sent one of the others to do something, but it probably wasn't to contact anyone concerning the ransom."

"I agree," Luke said. "I think Quanto is still with the girl. Plus, he is the only one capable of covering their trail."

"So we are restricted to following them and trusting to fortune."

Luke uttered a sigh. "Not much of a plan, but it's all we have."

"The first streams of daylight seeped through the cracks of her small prison and Cassie slowly uncurled from the fetal position. The oil slicker, which Quanto had provided to keep the water off during the night it had rained, she used for a ground blanket. Being fully dressed, with two other blankets, she did her best to weather the damp and cold in the small shelter. She moved stiffly, attempting to stretch out her legs. The action sent something scurrying out between a crack in the slab wall. There was some comfort that the visitor was a mouse and not a snake.

Sitting up, she brushed and folded the blankets. They were stiff with grime from being against the dirt floor, but she knew they would have to get her through at least one more night. Quanto had not mentioned a timetable, but she could see he was anxious to be done with the exchange. She had heard the other man complain of the delay too. Logically, each day they held her was one more day someone searching for her would have to find the hideout.

She ran her fingers through her hair, trying to put it in some kind of order, and making certain no insects had set up housekeeping. There was no escaping the dirt from the clinging earth or the grit and dust that seemed to ooze endlessly from the wood slats overhead. Her Sunday dress resembled a used cleaning rag, wrinkled and soiled beyond recognition, and she had dried muddy smears on both arms and on her knees.

She wondered if she dare ask Quanto if she could wash her clothing and maybe clean up. The deadly, rather taciturn man had already shown her more consideration than she would have ever thought possible. It was odd that he was the compassionate one of the kidnappers. From what John had told her, there was considerable proof that he had been the one to shoot and kill Preston in cold blood. She knew Preston had never carried a gun, didn't even own one in fact. He had some money in the house, but he wouldn't have put his own life at risk over a few dollars. Quanto had killed him without provocation. Only he knew the real reason why.

There was a thump at the door of the cabin and movement inside as someone walked over to open it. The third man had returned.

"It's about time." Quanto's voice reached Cassie. "We expected you back before dark last night."

The other replied, "There was a lot to do, Chief. I've spent the last forty-eight hours in the saddle. I'm going to eat something and then get a few hours' sleep."

"What happened to your face?"

There was a slight pause. "Oh that? Rode into a branch in the dark."

Quanto uttered a grunt of disbelief. "Sure you did. Looks more like scratch marks from a woman to me."

The second man laughed.

Cassie heard one of the men start working at the fireplace. He added wood and began to stoke up the fire. Cooking was something of a chore with only an open fireplace. There was a crude, rocklike shelf for the coffeepot, and the cooking pot was big enough to hold a meal for three or four. It limited what she could prepare, having to fix everything in a pot.

"You still kickin' in there, sweetheart?" Quanto's voice grated.

"I'm awake," she answered, mindful that he spoke to her in a crass manner for the benefit of his partners. "Do you wish for me to cook breakfast?"

"In a minute. These boys will step outside."

Before she could respond, one of the others spoke up. "This is just plain stupid, Chief. There ain't no need to hide from that female." After a pause, he added, "No one is going to catch up with us after we get the money."

"You want to take that chance?" the other man asked. "I've seen a story about one of those artist fellows working with the *Police Gazette*. They said he can draw about any man's picture from someone giving a description. I hear it's about as good as if they had an actual photograph."

"You'd be easy," the first one said with a sneer, "they'd only have to color the poster yellow."

"Hey! I'm not going to—"

"Shut up!" Quanto snarled at the two men. "You boys haul your duffs outside and tend the horses. I'll see that something is ready by the time you get finished up."

There was grumbling still, but the cabin door opened after a moment. A moment after it was closed behind them, Quanto pushed the wooden partition open for Cassie.

"Make it quick," he said, "the roosters are beginning to strut and crow."

"I don't wish to make trouble for you, Mr. Quanto."

He regarded her with a curious sort of frown. "We have some oatmeal and fixin's for cornpone or hoecakes. Whatever is easiest. Hustle up breakfast for the four of us and then, when chow is ready, you get back into your pen and stay there till I come back."

"You're leaving?"

"I have to keep an eye on what's going on."

She came into the main room of the shanty and straightened up. Her back ached from the confinement of the small hutch. After the short stretch, she began to sort out what she would use to prepare breakfast.

"May I ask you a question?" she asked while she began to mix up a batter.

"You can ask"—he put his hard eyes on her—"but it don't mean I'll answer."

"Why did you kill Preston? Did he put up a fight?"

Quanto stared at her long enough that she lowered her gaze. "I shouldn't have asked. I'm sorry."

"The man was a louse," he finally said. "Why should you care?"

"Actually"—she had a hard time finding the correct

words—"it was not a concern over Preston, I was trying to understand you."

"Don't bother."

"It's only that you've been very kind to me—under the circumstances."

"Don't let it go to your head, sweetheart. If the need arises, I'll kill you in a minute." His tone warned her to cease trying to analyze his moods or motives. "You've got fifteen minutes to fix the grub."

"All right."

"Soon as it's done, make a plate for yourself. I want you back into your hole before the others come back inside."

"It's . . ." She hesitated. "It's so very dirty."

"You'll have to suffer."

She didn't test his patience, hurrying to do as she was told. She had often made hoecakes for herself and her mother, but that had been on a stovetop griddle. She hoped the chore of cooking them over a fireplace was not going to be impossible.

Dexter Cline sat on the wagon seat and directed their horse, Pokey, to the head of the field of corn. As soon as the rest of the family finished the noon meal, his boy and three girls would start with sacks, picking the ears of corn from several rows at a time. As the bags were emptied into the wagon bed and the rows completed, he would pull the team ahead to keep pace. If the weather held, he reasoned they should be able to pick most of the field by dark. He and Tom Kensington had consigned all of the corn from their two farms for the same price. If their estimate was correct, they would have enough produce to fill an entire train car. The sale would bring an ample amount to pay up their accounts, hold them through the winter, and buy seed and supplies for next year's crops. Things were looking up.

He drove the wagon along the edge of the barbed-wire fence and stopped. He spied something fluttering among the weeds in the morning breeze. It appeared to be a piece of colored cloth. It was too far away from the house to have been an article of clothing from the clothesline.

"Probably just an old rag," he said aloud, climbing down from the wagon. He pulled two strands of wire apart so that he could slip through the fence, then he started toward the piece of flapping material.

After a few steps, he could see it more clearly. There was something there, something lying in the brush. A rush of fear invaded his chest. Dexter stopped dead in his tracks and stared, horror-stricken. It looked like a body!

Stumbling on trembling legs, he closed within a few feet. His heart pounded and the food he had just eaten tried to rise in his throat. He swallowed hard, set his teeth firmly, and took another step. The material he had seen was from a girl's dress. He recognized Sally Kensington, her lifeless eyes wide and staring. Her mouth was open in a final silent death cry. Dexter stumbled forward and dropped to his knees at her side.

"Dear Lord," he murmured, reaching out to take her hand. "No!"

But the girl's body was cold. Other than some dark bruises about her neck, he could not see another mark on her. Except for the gaping mouth, staring eyes, and contusions about her throat, she could have been sleeping.

Dexter dearly loved his own three daughters. He knew that Tom adored his Sally, whom he often called Little Princess. The loss was going to devastate the man.

"We about ready, Pa?" Jimmy had come up without him hearing. "What'cha doing over here in the—" He stopped in midsentence.

"Take Pokey and ride over to Tom's place. Tell him to

come at once.'' When Jimmy didn't answer, he turned and looked at him. The boy was completely shaken. His color was ashen, as if he was going to be sick. Dexter stood up to block the body from his sight and moved over to stand in front of his boy.

"Do what I tell you, son," he told him gently, controlling the shaking of his own voice. "Toss me a couple of the sacks from the back of the wagon, so I can cover her until we get a blanket."

"Who . . ." Jimmy had to swallow a sob. "Who would want to hurt Sally, Pa?"

"Only the lowest form of animal on earth, son. Now get a move on."

Jimmy hurried over to the wagon and retrieved a couple sacks. He tossed them to Dexter, then he quickly began to unharness Pokey.

Dexter carefully covered the girl with the burlap bags. Tears burned his eyes as he knelt on the ground next to her. She had been a vibrant and cheerful girl, with a zest for fun and life. Who could have done something so brutal?

Chapter Thirteen

Lariquette turned over the last card and Cracker tossed in his hand. "You got to be cheating! You ain't lost a hand in the past hour!"

"You wouldn't exactly earn a living as a riverboat gambler, sonny. Maybe we should play some five-card stud. The only strategy in that is the betting."

"I'm tired of playing cards. I want to get this over with."

"Quanto has to check around and see what's going on. If I read men correctly, he will have some information for us when he gets back."

"Yeah, but we have to sit and wait, Frenchy. I feel like I'm waiting for the hangman."

"Keep your voice down," Lariquette said under his breath, "and don't use names."

"Frenchy ain't your name."

"It would be enough to link me with this job."

"Oh, yeah, as if no one is going to figure we joined with Quanto on this deal. The three of us escaped together. It stands to reason that we would all be in on the same job."

Lariquette fingered the twin scratch marks on his cheek and stared at the rear of the cabin, trying to penetrate the darkness of the attached hutch. It was impossible, for the slats were too closely knit. He lowered his voice to a mere whisper.

"I'll tell you what I think, my friend. I think it's a mistake to let the woman live." He leaned across the table and bore into Cracker with hard eyes. "Without her, no one can prove we were in on this deal."

"She hasn't seen us."

"You think she's stupid? Those cracks in the wall are big enough to see through in a dozen places. You can bet she's seen us."

"Maybe."

"Even if she has been too frightened to look, she's heard us talking, put out dishes for us at mealtime. She knows there are three of us. If we're caught, it'll be a short step off of a long drop with a noose around our necks."

"Quanto says no one will ever catch us. His escape plan sounds foolproof, two more sets of horses, spaced nearly sixty miles apart, then we grab the train and get off at Evanston. Ain't no posse in the world going to keep up with us. You done set it up by yourself!"

"I admit, the escape is well thought out. But it's after we make our getaway that bothers me. You want to hide out the rest of your life?"

Cracker shrugged his shoulders. "I don't see no other choice."

"With my share, I can open up a casino somewhere. You think I can do that with the law still looking for me?"

"You know how Quanto feels about that. He says if we kill the woman, the law will never let us rest."

"If we let her live, she'll always be there to point her finger at us."

"I couldn't kill no woman, Frenchy. Besides, Quanto wouldn't allow it."

"Quanto won't allow it," Lariquette complained. "You think too small, Cracker. We would have a lot more money to split between us without Quanto."

Cracker's face paled at the mere thought. He licked his lips and cast a nervous glance at the lean-to. He barely whispered, "I don't know, Frenchy. He's a scary sort, about as deadly as any man I ever seen. He wouldn't be an easy man to kill."

"Give a thought as to how you would spend twenty-five thousand dollars, my friend. With so much money, you could go to Mexico and live like a king for the rest of your life."

The glimmer that shone within Cracker's eyes revealed that he found the number impressive. Quanto was offering them a third, which was certainly fair, but half? He leaned back, as if to consider the options.

"How would we handle it?"

"We'll bide our time for now." Lariquette's gaze went beyond Cracker, resting again on the wall. He had seen few women that were as desirable as Cassandra Hytower. With her poise and charm, she was something special. If not for Quanto, he would have tried his hand at winning her over.

Not that Cassandra would ever fall in love with him, but most people would do about anything necessary to survive. When the time came, he would allow her to believe that being nice to him would save her life. She would yield willingly, eager to satisfy his every desire, using her charms to dissuade him from disposing of her. He would allow her to think she had succeeded, at least until he grew tired of her company. There was no room in his future for a permanent woman, especially one who could testify against him in court.

"Once we get the ransom money, we'll take care of Quanto." He bore into Cracker with his steellike gaze. "You in or out?"

The skinny man cracked his knuckles nervously. "I'm in."

Quanto cut a telegraph wire and sent a message to Broken Spoke. Then he continued on to town, cautiously circling around to approach from the opposite direction. He picketed his horse a half-mile out and stealthily entered on foot. A man who used shadows and any form of concealment as well as any Indian, he crept up to Bunion's corrals without so much as alerting a dog. Once he was among the horses at the livery, it was not a difficult chore to slip into the barn and climb up to the loft. He intended to get a couple hours' sleep and then sneak around to listen at doors and windows once it was dark. He would seek out Cole and John Fairbourn. Other than Luke Mallory, they would be the men who would control the actions of the town. As for Mallory, his little ranch was too far across the valley to chance a visit.

Quanto had not yet dozed off when he heard a ruckus out in the street. He peered through a crack between the wooden slabs of the hayloft, curious as to why dozens of townspeople were gathered around Dexter Cline's rig. As luck would have it, the wagon had rolled to a stop in front of the jail, only a couple hundred feet up the street. Cole was there to wave his cane and keep the people back.

"Was it them stinkin' kidnappers?" someone called.

"Form a posse!" another cried. "We'll hunt them dirty varmints to the ends of the earth!"

"We'll draw and quarter the murdering scum!" joined in a third.

"Hold on, people!" Cole shouted them down. "We don't know anything yet. Dexter found the girl out by his place. She's been strangled, but that's all we know for sure."

"It was them darned, vile kidnappers!" a man bellowed. "Who else would kill her?"

Quanto felt a hollow sensation in his stomach, followed at once with a tightness that burned within his chest. A girl had been killed? Was it Cassie? Had Lariquette lost his mind and murdered their hostage? He pressed against the wooden partition and tried to see the body.

"She was only a kid!" a woman sobbed. "Just a child!"

"Why would they kill Sally?" another asked.

"To make sure we knew what would happen to the Hy-tower woman if we tried anything," another replied. "This is sure enough a warning not to try nothing!"

Quanto was relieved to discover the body in the wagon was not Cassandra, but he still experienced rage over the death of an innocent girl. "Lariquette!" he hissed the name under his breath.

"Put the girl's body in the icehouse until we can make arrangements for a funeral," Cole instructed. "There's nothing can be done for her now."

"Why did they do this?" Tom Kensington lamented, the grief and anguish thick in his voice. "Mont and Fairbourn were going to pay the money. They didn't have to kill my little girl."

Cartwell Devine put an arm around his shoulders. "We're all real sorry, Tom. She was a beautiful little girl, always sweet and smiling. We all share the pain of your loss.''

Tom shook his head sorrowfully as Cartwell led him over to the saloon. ''A drink might be in order,'' he said gently. ''Come with me.''

Quanto backed away from the crack, sick inside. He thought of the scratch marks on Lariquette's face. A tree branch! the man had said. The slimy snake had attacked and killed the Kensington girl.

Doubling his fists in vehemence, Quanto swore under his breath. He recalled his first impression of the Frenchman. He had thought the man was nothing more than a fast-talking back shooter. Cheating at cards would not have gotten him a five-year prison sentence, but pulling his gun first would have had an impact on any self-defense claim. He had suggested that they kill Cassandra too. The ruthless buzzard was the lowest form of human being, a man without a soul or conscience. The story of a branch hitting him in the face had been a clumsy excuse to cover being scratched while killing the girl. He had sacrificed her as a warning, to convince the people of Broken Spoke that they were serious.

Quanto gave a cynical grunt, thinking how the murder might backfire. Not only was it foolish and unnecessary, but it might work against them. The townspeople might decide the abductors intended to kill Cassandra, whether they paid the ransom or not. If so, they would mount a rescue attempt, rather than forking over the money.

Along the same lines, if Lariquette was willing to murder a helpless victim to make a point, he likely had entertained ideas about killing the hostage. He couldn't do that, unless he also planned to get rid of Quanto and take all of the money for himself. Quanto vowed to keep a sharp eye for any kind of trick.

Sitting silently, he did a little contemplating about how and when the Frenchman would make his move. With the possibility of a trick or ambush during the exchange, the man would bide his time until they had the ransom money in hand. Quanto had not explained that part of the scheme to him, so he was reasonably safe until after the trade.

Regret and a longing entered his being. He hated the thought that his actions had been responsible for the death of Tom's daughter. He also regretted having taken Cassandra hostage. He had put her life in jeopardy, and she had never said or did anything to hurt him. Indeed, she had always treated him in a civil manner.

He remembered how he had often admired her discreetly, while working for her power-hungry husband. There had been a number of times when he had watched her from a distance, simply enjoying the way she moved. Cassandra had asked why he had killed Preston. He had not answered the question, but he was well aware of the truth. Preston was the only man he had ever killed in cold blood. He didn't rationalize or make excuses for the act. The pompous swine had beaten and abused Cassandra, then given her away as if she were a monetary award. He deserved a bullet.

Still thinking of the woman, Quanto knew he was not the first to be beguiled by Cassandra. Yarrow had been so smitten by her it cost him his own life and resulted in Quanto being captured. Another man in her life, John Fairbourn, was the most decent and moral man in the valley. Yet he had been ready to sell his soul for a mere touch of the lady's hand. There was no explaining what it was about Cassandra that so affected men. She was attractive, but so were a good many other women. Maybe it was the sparkle that shone in her eyes, a zest from deep inside, a special elegance that radiated from within. It made a man want to protect and covet her affection. When he gazed into her eyes, he wanted to possess her.

Quanto grunted to himself, firmed his resolve, and shook the vision of Cassandra out of his head. Dreams of that sort were for men without a grasp of reality. He kept watch for a few more minutes while the people mingled about in the street. They were not organized, lacking a real leader for something like a manhunt. He figured they would send for Luke Mallory or possibly one of the ranchers for assistance. This new development was going to force him to move his plan ahead without delay. It also ruined any chance of prowling the streets and listening at windows or closed doors. He could ill afford for anyone to find his trail. They might jump to the conclusion that he had killed the Kensington girl.

Grief once more bit into his soul at the thought. The kidnapping of Cassandra had been the worst thing he ever did. He had put a few men in the ground, even one or two who didn't deserve to be killed. But he had never harmed a woman or a child. It was of paramount importance that nothing happen to Cassandra. He had brought Cracker and the Frenchman into this. He would have to make certain Lariquette paid for his deed and the girl was returned unharmed, no matter what the cost!

John heard the rider enter the yard. He was to the door before Mont could even get out of his chair. "It's Bunion!"

The scrawny man got down from his horse, gave the reins a cinch at the hitching post, and came up to the porch. "How about something to drink?" he asked. "This here riding about like an errand boy makes a man thirsty."

John stepped back to allow him to enter the house. Mont was already pouring a drink from a bottle of brandy.

Bunion took a big swig and about choked on it. "Whoa!" he sputtered. "This ain't whiskey!"

"I don't keep whiskey in the house," Mont replied. "I only have a little wine with my evening meals."

"Ain't hardly civilized, if'n you ask me."

"Is there some news? Have you heard from the kidnappers?" John asked.

"Two things," he said morosely. "One is bad, and one is worse."

"What are you talking about, Bunion?"

"First off, we got us a telegraph message. It wasn't from no nearby town, so we figure Quanto must have ridden over to the wire and climbed a pole or something. Anyhow, it said that you was to be the one to bring the money for Cassandra Hytower, John. The next message is going to arrive tomorrow and say where to take the ransom. At that point, you'll find directions for getting Mrs. Hytower back."

"Do we trust him?" Mont asked.

"I don't think we have a choice."

"All right, we'll follow the man's instructions. Any word from Mallory?"

Bunion's head rotated back and forth. "No, but he and that smart-mouthed Injun still have some time left. With some luck, they might have run them down before we get the wire."

"Any idea what time we can expect the next message?" John asked.

"Tomorrow is all it said."

"Will the money be here by then?"

"Wells Fargo promised delivery on the morning stage," Mont replied. "I'll need to be in town to sign for that strongbox."

"I'll have my buggy ready first thing, Mont. We'll be in town waiting for word."

"All right," Mont agreed. Then he looked back at Bunion. "You said two things. What's the other one?"

"There's been a murder." Bunion's scrawny shoulders bowed and he ducked his head sorrowfully. "Sally Kensington was found strangled to death."

John was stunned to silence. Mont had to take a chair, as if the weight of the news was too heavy to bear while standing.

"Dexter found her body, right near his place. Tom didn't know she was missing. She had told him she was going to walk into town the afternoon before and help work on Timony's wedding dress. He assumed that she spent the night in Broken Spoke. We asked Mrs. Devine, but Sally never showed up."

"You think Quanto did it?" Mont asked. "Is this his way of getting our attention?"

"I don't see why Quanto would feel that was necessary," John replied. "We already know he is a capable killer. What good would killing an innocent girl do for him?"

"It might be to send a message that we pay or else," Bunion said. "Killing Sally could be his way of telling us he was serious about us paying the ransom."

"Did they find any clues to the killer? Do we know it was Quanto?"

"Cully Deeks is making a check of the area. I'd guess he is as good a man as we have for that sort of thing, what with Mallory and the Injun up chasing after Quanto's trail."

"I'll ride over and have a look too," John offered. "Tom is going to be shattered. He thought the world of Sally."

"It's a sad day when a little girl is murdered," Bunion said softly, "a sad day indeed."

Chapter Fourteen

Cully Deeks spent two hours searching around for any clues. The grass showed where Dexter had pulled the wagon. He also found a number of prints, but he didn't know how many people had walked around the area. There was no blood, no evidence of a struggle at all. Dexter and his kids had put the girl into their wagon and gone for help. He could see nothing but their tracks.

Having arrived after the fact, he had not examined the girl's body. Dexter told him the only marks were about her neck. As she was fully dressed, it appeared on the surface that she had not been violated.

Why kill the girl? he wondered. Did Quanto really think it was necessary to make everyone take him seriously? Was he sending a message, or did this murder have nothing to do with the kidnapping?

He was circling the area as he tried to make sense of the murder. Suddenly, he stopped in midstep. Beneath some flattened-over grass, there was an imprint of a man's boot on the ground. It was deep, as if the man was either quite large, or he had been carrying something heavy. Cully searched around for a few minutes, but there was only one track. It was impossible to know the man's direction, but it was obvious the killer had carried the girl over to the edge of Cline's cornfield.

A rider approached down from the trail and stopped at the fence. Cully looked over to see John Fairbourn.

"Find anything?" John asked.

"One print that might belong to the killer. It looks as if he brought the girl's body up near the road, so we would be sure to find her."

John dismounted and ground-reined his horse. It was trained to stay where he left it, so it didn't move when he climbed through the fence and walked over to examine the lone mark on the ground.

"Proportion is about right," John said, staring at the print. "Quanto is a fair-sized man."

"This field of meadow grass did a good job of hiding any prints. This here is the only one I've found. I'd say the killer carried the girl for some distance." He pointed to the barbed-wire fence. "Tom said Sally was going to town. She could take the shortest route by crossing the fields and entering town from the east. There was no need for her to cross the stream to this side."

"Ruthless scum!" John said with a growl. "I knew Quanto was cold-blooded, but this is the lowest a man could sink."

"Guess he wanted to be sure we wouldn't try any tricks at the exchange."

John stood erect and paused to stare out over the wide expanse beyond the farms. "A brutal act like this adds to our worries about Mrs. Hytower, Deeks. If Mallory and that

Indian get too close, those ruthless vultures might decide to kill her.''

''The Indian is supposed to be the best, John. And you know Luke won't take any chances until they are in a position to get her away safe.''

''Think they are having more luck than us?''

Cully thought for a moment. ''I don't know, but I have to wonder if this was Quanto, or was it one of the others with him? I only met him a time or two, but I didn't read him to be the kind of man to kill a woman.''

''He shot Preston in cold blood.''

''Yeah, but that was during a robbery.''

''The man wasn't even armed.''

''I know, but there's other things here that don't make sense. Like, why would Quanto strangle the girl? I wouldn't figure the breed to kill someone in such a way. He always carried a knife.''

''Some people scream when a blade is shoved into their body, Deeks. Strangling was a quiet way of killing her.''

''Maybe, but I'll bet Quanto knows where to stick a person so they can't draw enough breath to scream.''

''You've a point there. Anything else?''

''Not much. Like I said, the guy carried Sally's body up where it would be found. I haven't been able to find where he left his horse.''

''That much sounds like Quanto. I'm surprised you found his tracks.''

''Only one, John, and it might not even belong to our killer.''

John took a long look around, pausing to stare at the nearby fields, off toward the Queen place, which was now home for the Ingersol family, then diverted his gaze to the Dakota Creek. A man like Quanto could have been fifty feet from their position and they would not have been able to see him. Sally had probably not even known she was being stalked until it was too late to run.

"It's a real shame," he said softly. "Tom dearly loved that girl."

"She was a sweet little thing," Cully agreed. "One day soon, we'll make Quanto pay."

John gave a solemn nod. "Guess there's nothing for me to do here. Without a trail to follow, you don't need my help."

"Sorry, but I'd say the killer got away clean. If it was Quanto, I'm not surprised there's no trail."

"I am to see that he pays for his crimes, Deeks. Once Cassandra is safe, I'm going to hook up with Mallory and that Indian tracker. We'll darn well follow Quanto and his pals to the ends of the earth. There won't be a rock big enough or far enough away for them to hide under."

"You can count me in on the hunt too, John."

The image of Sally was strong, always smiling and laughing. The biggest flirt around, she was still adored by everyone in Broken Spoke. Her cheerful enthusiasm for life would be sorely missed.

"I'll see you later, Deeks. I've got to pick up Mont early and be in town at first light. I'll be there waiting when we get word again."

"Luck" was the only word Cully had to offer.

John went back to his horse and mounted up. He was filled with a foreboding gloom, a fear that Quanto would kill Cassie, even if they paid the ransom. It gnawed at his insides like a rat chewing through a grain sack. He was growing haggard, having barely managed to eat or sleep since the kidnapping. Someone said that worrying did no good, but trying not to worry was like trying not to blink. He had to keep thinking positively. They would get her back. Everything would turn out okay.

He neck-reined his mount in the direction of the Hytower place. A death with no clues, a kidnapping by a ruthless killer, and no word from Mallory. It was real tough to keep up a hopeful outlook.

Darkness covered the land and it was another meal of beans and hard rolls. The same questions had been running through Luke's mind since they set out to follow him. How did Quanto intend to get word to Broken Spoke and the man with the money? How did he plan to escape? How would the exchange be made?

As they settled down for a few hours' sleep, he spoke of his concern to the Indian.

"Maybe this Quanto is going to use the mail to send his demands," Joe suggested. "I mean, he has to get his demands into town some way, unless he contacts one of the outlying ranches. He could slip in and leave a note, but there would be fresh tracks to follow. Hiding evidence of travel like the man did on this trail takes a lot of time."

"The mail would be too slow, and he couldn't be sure they would get the letter on time. He would need to . . ." Luke sat up straight. "A telegraph! That's what he would need!"

"Send a wire with instructions?"

"Sure! It makes sense."

"How would he accomplish that?"

"There is a line running to Rimrock. It followed the old cross-country trail, before they changed where the stage crosses the creek. It's a few miles east of here."

"Do you think Quanto knows how to tap into the telegraph wire?"

"I'm betting that man knows a good many tricks."

"How does it help us, even if he did send a message over the wire?"

"There would be a recent set of tracks from his horse."

"Your presumption is *if* he can use the telegraph, and *if* he has already sent his message. It sounds like a big gamble, paleface."

"At the rate we're moving, we aren't going to find their camp before time is up for the ransom to be paid. Wells Fargo will have the money here by late today or early tomorrow. If they are planning to have the girl at the exchange, they'll have relocated to a point where they can make the trade and then escape. We're going to be too late."

Joe took a general sweep with a wave of his arm. "You pointed out that there isn't anything for a hundred miles out this way. Where are they going to escape to?"

"I don't know, but the Union Pacific Railroad is only a day's ride south of here. Quanto will want to get out of Wyoming as quickly as possible. I'm sure he's picked a route for his flight which is away from any pursuit. I'd guess the missing rider has been arranging that part of their plan."

"All right," Joe allowed, "but even if all of your guesswork is correct, what do we do about it?"

"Come morning, you keep the two Ingersol boys with you and continue following the trail. I'll cut across to the telegraph line and start following it. All I need is to see a place where a man can climb up and interrupt the line. It's a good bet that he cut the wire and left it down. Once the ransom is paid, Cole couldn't send out word to head them off. It makes sense."

"I'll wish you luck now, paleface," Joe offered. "You're going to need it."

Luke felt the urge to ride out, even though it would soon be dark. His patience was gone. They were running out of time and had accomplished nothing. The chance of cutting

Quanto's trail or rescuing Cassandra was remote at best, but he had come up with one option. Splitting up would double their odds at finding something. That was the best shot they had at the moment.

Chapter Fifteen

Edna eyed Amber with suspicion. "I seen that cow-sitter pass by again last evening. You was tight-lipped last night and all day today. I'm tired of waiting for you to say something about it."

"Kind of slipped my mind, Ma."

"A night and whole day passes and you ain't thought of it, huh?" She uttered a cynical grunt. "You sure there ain't nothing going on that I ought to be aware of?"

"No, Ma," Amber replied. "Mr. Deeks claimed he only come down to the creek to water his horse."

"And you believed him?"

Amber could not prevent a smile from coming to surface. "I figure he was trying to impress upon me his desire to come courting again."

"Sneaking down behind my back ain't the way to win favor."

"No, Ma, I done told him as much."

"Where was you?" she asked Leland.

"Fishing, Ma," he answered quickly. "I was fishing, like you told me I could do."

Edna eased up on her inquisition. "It's dark outside, son. You best take one last look at the animals for the night."

"Yeah, Ma," he said, hurrying over to pick up his hat. Then he went out the door.

"He misses Ray," she said quietly. "Don't know what that boy would do without his brother to watch over him."

"You're right about that, Ma," Amber agreed. "I don't remember him ever being so rueful and quiet. He ain't said two words all day."

"Should have kept Donny here and sent him with Ray. He would have been happy, and easy as much help if it came to a fight."

"You think he'll ever find himself a girl, or will he spend the rest of his life living under the same roof as you or Ray?"

Edna sighed. "The boy is a working fool. A woman could sure do worse."

"Yeah, but he don't think real quick. It would have to be a gal who wanted control of their lives. She would be the one what handled the money and such."

"Small price to pay for the dedication Leland would give her."

Edna was silent a few moments. When she spoke again, there was a new concern etched into her granite features. "I don't want you going to the creek without Leland for the next few days."

"Why not? I won't be seeing that cowboy again, not unless he comes here first. He promised me."

"It ain't that."

"What then?"

A rare concern swept across Edna's usually stern face.

"There's been a murder," she answered sedately, "one of our neighbors."

Amber sucked in her breath. "A murder?"

"Girl about your age," Edna went on. "I didn't want to mention it in front of Leland. He is too much a kid to understand such things."

"Who was it?"

"Sally Kensington, girl from the place east of here. She was strangled and left near the main trail. Dexter Cline, one of the other nearby farmers, he and his wife come by on the wagon this afternoon whilst you and Leland were filling the water barrel. They think it has to do with the kidnapping of that other woman, the one from the Hytower ranch."

"Why would the kidnappers kill another girl?"

"Must have been to make sure everyone took them serious. Anyway, if you need to go to the creek for water, washing or laundry, I want you to take Leland with you. If you want to take a bath, you only got to tell him to keep his back turned. You know he won't look." At her silence, Edna prompted, "You hear me?"

"Yeah, Ma."

"When is the cowboy supposed to come courting?" she changed the subject.

"He didn't say."

"You like him, do you?"

"He's got a way of looking at me that I find rather fetching."

"Maybe like you was a big steak and he was starving?"

Amber laughed. "Kind of."

"You don't know nothing about him."

"I know I can run faster than he can."

"He chased you?"

"We had a race. I won."

Edna shook her head. "You always was able to hold your own with the boys."

"He said that a man and woman shouldn't compete against one another, that they was supposed to work together side by side."

"Courting words."

"You and Pa was like that. I remember how he always ran the family, but you ran the house. He never made a decision without you and he first talked it over."

"Your pa was a good man. We never went without food on the table or a roof over our heads, not in the twenty-five years we was married. A woman can't ask no more of her man than that."

"No, Ma."

"Been a stray dog hanging around the back door today," Edna said, changing the subject. "I thought about feeding it some wolfsbane and getting rid of it, but . . ." She gave a subtle shrug of her shoulders. "Maybe I'm getting old and sentimental. It wouldn't hurt to have a dog around, not if there might be a killer wandering round."

"I agree."

"Step out and ask Leland if he wants me to save any of these scraps for later. If not I'll throw it to the dog."

Amber quickly left the house. She started toward the corral, but saw Leland over near the woodpile. As she changed her direction, he heard her coming. Oddly he stuck something quickly under the corner of a log.

"What are you doing over here?" she asked.

"Nothing," he replied quickly, "I ain't doing nothing."

"Ma wants to know if you'll be hungry later."

"Not me. I'm full up."

"She says there's been a dog hanging around the yard today. You seen it?"

"He allowed for me to pet him this morning," Leland said. "Don't know where he is now."

"Once Ma feeds him, I expect we'll have ourselves another member of the family. Would you like that?"

"Yeah, I guess."

Amber wondered at his lack of enthusiasm. "Okay then, I'll tell Ma to put out the leftovers for him."

"Yeah, okay."

Amber paused a moment. "Is there something wrong, Leland?"

"No, Sis. There ain't nothing wrong."

She went back to the house, but his strange behavior puzzled her. He had tucked something under that log, but what would he hide from her?

As was her habit, Edna awakened Amber first. Not only did Amber help with breakfast, but getting out of bed first allowed her a degree of privacy from the boys. With all of them sleeping in the same room, privacy was impossible most of the time.

"Bring in a little wood for the fire," Edna said in a hushed voice. "Once we get the stove going good, you can dip some water out of the barrel. We have enough coffee for one meal. We'll have it this morning."

"All right, Ma," Amber replied, pulling on her Levi's under her sleeping gown. She didn't think Leland would feign sleeping and peek at her, but from the time she entered her teenage years, she didn't feel comfortable dressing in the same room with her brothers. When she had learned that Uncle Miller and his two sons had been killed, and the farm had been left to Edna, she had hoped for a house with two or three rooms. It was hard growing up without a bit of solitude, lacking the dignity of getting dressed without sharing the same room with three boys, never even being allowed the seclusion of taking a bath without fear of one of the boys walking in on her.

Thinking along such lines, she made her exit from the house. She could reason that the circumstances were the same for the boys, but Amber didn't feel that boys required as much privacy as a girl, especially when they had three-to-one odds in their favor.

As she approached the woodpile, she remembered Leland's strange behavior the previous night. She cast a look over her shoulder, to be certain he was not up and out of the house yet. Then she ventured over to where she had seen him standing. Careful not to disturb the wood in that part of the stack, she lifted a corner of each log or chunk of wood and began to search.

Leland was often like an overgrown child. He had found an injured squirrel once and tended it for a week, before it was well enough to escape. He also liked to make things, surprises for Edna or another family member, usually Ray. She wondered if he had started work on a project or had found himself another tiny pet.

Moving a piece of wood, she discovered his precious stash. Amber sucked in her breath at the sight. It was different from anything she had expected. She reached out to touch it, but heard the door open. She hastily shoved the block into place and knelt down to start gathering an armload of small tender.

Leland came around the corner of the house. His expression was anxious, as if he was frightened of something. It set off a warning signal in Amber's head. She forced a smile of greeting to her face, concealing the alarm she felt.

"If you came to help, you're a little late, Big Brother. I've got enough wood for the stove."

Leland stopped in his tracks, his features showing a mixture of confusion and panic. "I'm supposed to get the wood,'' he said hesitantly. "Ma says I should do it. It's my chore."

"You can sure have it." She again hid any misgivings. "The wood is too rough against the bare skin of my arms."

"It's my chore," he said a second time. "I'll do it, Sis. Leave if for me."

"Sure thing, Leland, it's your chore."

He looked around the yard. "Did you see my dog yet this morning?"

"Your dog?"

"Ma said I can have him. I'm going to call him Pepper, 'cause he is black."

"Probably off chasing a rabbit or something. If Ma fed him, he'll be back."

"Ma said I could have him as my very own," Leland repeated. "I've never had me a dog before."

"Good for you, Leland."

"You think Ray will let me keep him?"

"Sure."

He began to get his color back. "I'll cut some wood now. It's my chore."

"All right. I'll call you when breakfast is ready."

"Okay."

Amber walked past him and went into the house. Edna was stoking the fire and adding a few chips to the cast-iron stove. For a moment, she about told her what she had found. Then she thought better of it. She didn't want Leland thinking she would spy on him, and Edna could be very blunt and forthright at times. She would likely scold Leland for keeping a secret. Once Ray got back, Amber would speak to him. He was best able to deal with Leland. He could get answers without hurting the big boy's feelings.

Chapter Sixteen

The sun had only been up an hour when Bunion arrived to fetch John, Mont and Cartwell, who had all been having breakfast at the Ace High Saloon. The three of them joined Bunion and hurried over to the jail. They stood and listened while Cole finished scribbling down the words from the tapping of the telegraph. When it stopped, he picked up the sheet of paper and handed it to them.

John took the paper, his heart hammering wildly as he stared at the writing.

"What's it say?" Bunion asked.

"Yeah," Cartwell joined in, "read it aloud."

"I can't," John replied, pausing to turn the sheet upside down. "I can't make it out."

"Fer the love of . . . you telling me you can't read?" Cole snapped the question.

"Only English. I have no idea what language you wrote this message in."

He grunted and snatched the paper back. "Harlot has got more sense than most people in this town."

"Bet your cat can't read it either," John shot back. "If you can't write legibly, why don't you print the letters?"

Cole looked at the sheet. "Plain as day, it says to take the money to the northwest corner of Big George's ranch. There's a place where a single cedar tree stands on a knoll." He squinted at John. "You know the place?"

"Deeks or Big George can point me the right way."

"Says there will be another note with directions." He still appeared miffed over John not being able to make out his handwriting. "You're to come alone. Hope you can read Quanto's hand without me being there to decipher for you."

"This is it," Bunion said from behind them. "No word from Mallory, so we have to figure him and the Injun ain't had no luck."

Mont retrieved the money from the jail cell, where Cole had kept it during the wait. "Here it is," he said, handing the satchel to John, "fifty thousand dollars. Take the money and bring Cassandra home safe."

"I've got two horses at the hitching post," John told the others. "Like I said, I'll swing by Big George's place and make sure I can find that knoll."

"We ought to have someone to watch John's back," Bunion said. "What's to stop them boys from killing him and taking the money?"

"There's no reason, so long as we do what Quanto wants," Cartwell replied.

"Tell that to Tom Kensington," Bunion shot back. "They killed his girl just to let us know how serious they were."

"I'm going alone," John said firmly. "No tricks, just me. It's the way it has to be."

"I don't like it, son," Cole told him, "but I reckon we don't have any other choice."

Cartwell offered his hand. "Good luck, John."

John shook hands all around, then he was out the door. Somewhere out there was a frightened young woman, a woman he knew was waiting for him to come for her. She had likely suffered all manner of terror and abuse while being held hostage. It was up to him to bring her home safely. And he would darn well get her back, even if it meant killing each and every one of the kidnappers.

Mounting his horse, he took the second animal in tow. Quanto had taken a horse for Cassie, but that didn't mean they would leave her one. There was no telling how the man had planned his escape, so John had to be prepared for anything.

Luke had been on his horse since daylight. From the direction of the kidnappers, he made a mental calculation of where they could intercept the telegraph line. Once he reached the string of poles, he began to follow the trail north, away from Broken Spoke. Several hours had passed, when he spied a downed line. His guess had been correct!

He rushed over to the spot and studied the scene. It was Quanto, it had to be! The man had used the wire to contact Broken Spoke. On the ground, he could see tracks of a recent horse and rider. From the looks of it, the man had come across the open country to intercept the telegraph line, where it was strung toward Wheatland. Studying the marks, it appeared the rider had then gone off toward Big George's most distant grazing range. That gave him a moment to pause and do some contemplating.

If the tracks were Quanto's, he could follow the trail and possibly overtake the man. Either that, or he might be able to observe the ransom exchange from a distance. His presence could be a deciding factor if there were any kind of trick. The problem was, what if Cassandra was not there? Quanto was no fool. He would not give up the girl without making sure he first had the money in hand and a good headstart on any pursuit. Luke decided his first concern was to get the girl back safely. If he showed his hand and Cassandra was being held at a separate location, he would have wasted their only opportunity for a surprise.

Alternatively, he could backtrack in the direction from which Quanto had come. With luck, he might locate their hideout. If he got there ahead of Quanto, there was a chance he might be able to free the girl and then set a trap for the breed. Such an action would require taking care of the other man or men involved in the kidnapping and possibly risking Cassandra's life. Alone, the odds were not that much in his favor. As this was likely the day of the exchange, the abductors were bound to be on the alert.

A third option was to make a heated run back to get Injun Joe and the Ingersol boys. With four of them, there would be a much better chance of being successful in a move against the hideout and in effecting a rescue. The problem with such a plan was the distance and time a strategy like that would require. An hour or two to find the three men, another hour to return to the telegraph line, then however long it took to trace Quanto's trail back to his hideout. It would be late afternoon before they could manage such a feat. By that time, it might be too late to catch them.

Luke looked over the terrain while trying to choose an option. If he tried to follow Quanto, the man might spot him. If he backtracked him, there was a chance the man would come across his tracks and overtake him from behind. Even if he found the hideout, he would be facing one or two men, with Quanto still on the loose. However, to risk the time needed to get Joe was to possibly allow the ransom exchange to take place. Once they had their money, the job of overtaking them would be difficult, if not impossible. Quanto would have presumably given a great deal of thought to their escape. The chances of catching them were not all that good.

"So what's the best move?" he asked aloud.

With a grim determination, he decided to backtrack Quanto. It was probable that the man would take a different route back to the hiding place. With any luck, he would not discover that someone was on his trail. If Luke could get there ahead of him, he might come up with a plan to rescue the hostage. If he arrived too late, and the kidnappers and Cassandra were gone, he would have a fresh trail to follow.

After the first couple hours, Luke had to admire Quanto. The man had left a false path in two different places. Twice, after losing the trail, he had been forced to make a circle to pick up the tracks of the horse. The breed also rode in alternating zigzag routes, so it was impossible to predict the direction from which way he had come. It made tracking him both slow and difficult. He began to wonder about the wisdom of his plan. At his slow pace, he might reach the hideout long after everyone was gone!

Some twenty miles to the west, Joe and the two Ingersol boys had stopped. Something new had been added to the trail they had been following.

"What you looking at, Indian Joe?" Donny asked. "You been staring at the ground in that same spot for fifteen minutes."

Joe pointed off to the south. "I think the man who left at the creek has returned to join the others. His horse was the one with the missing shoe."

"What's that mean?"

"These tracks were made after the rain, probably early yesterday, and this guy isn't trying to hide his tracks. I'd say we have us a fresh trail to follow."

"You think so?"

Joe decided that neither of the Ingersol boys would ever become college professors. He hid the sarcasm from his voice, however. "When this guy left the creek, it was off in the direction of the railroad or possibly one of the nearby towns. I would wager he went to secure or prepare an escape route. It's a good bet he wanted to be back with the others for the exchange of their hostage for the money. Not a lot of trust among thieves."

"Then he's headed toward their hiding place!"

"Exactly."

"So why are you standing there like you're putting down roots?" Ray asked. "Let's get after him!"

"We can move quicker now, but we must be more careful. We can't simply ride up to the hideout. If they see us coming, they might set an ambush or even kill the woman."

"All right, we'll still take it careful," Ray promised. "You lead and we'll follow."

Joe got onto his horse. It was the first time since picking up the trail of the kidnappers that he had been able to follow without being on foot. His eyes searched the rolling hills ahead. This man had not tried to cover his tracks. He was not the leader, and neither was he as careful as the half-breed tracker. This man had felt perfectly safe to ride in the open and not worry about leaving a trail. A man like Quanto would never be so careless.

"What's the bonus if we get the girl back?" Donny asked.

"I'm working by the day," Joe answered. "No one said anything to me about a bonus."

"Yeah, well, you're probably not getting two dollars a day either," Ray bragged. "Being an Indian, bet you're working for half that."

Joe whistled. "Mallory is paying you boys two dollars a day? Each?"

Ray was smug. "Advantage of being a white man, Indian Joe."

"You're right on that point, boys," he replied. "I'd never have dared ask for two dollars a day."

John first spied the tree, then saw the paper tacked to it. He swept over the area with his eyes but saw only the flutter of a bird in a nearby sage as it jumped from one branch to another. He rode up to the knoll and retrieved the note. It read:

LEAVE THE MONEY. GO TO TWIN ROCKS TWO MILES EAST. THERE ARE DIRECTIONS TO FIND MRS. HYTOWER. IF YOU TRY ANY TRICKS, WE WILL KILL HER.

John felt uneasy, knowing Quanto was close enough to be watching him. He removed the satchel from his horse and placed it by the tree. Then he was back in the saddle, with the lead rope to the other mount in hand. He started east, checking the ground ahead of him. Quanto had left a readable trail, so he would be able to find the twin rocks without any trouble.

The half-breed's plan was simple, but it was also smart. There could be no tricks. If the money wasn't there, or if he saw someone following after John, he had time to return to where the girl was and either kill her or move her. Even if he were captured, before he could return, there were still his partners. Cassandra would not be released until Quanto was there with the money. After that, John suspected, the man had set up an escape plan that would outdistance any pursuit. John's only course of action was to follow the instructions in the letter.

Chapter Seventeen

Cassie was shocked when one of the men working with Quanto entered the hutch. He and the other man had been careful to guard their identity, yet he was now showing himself.

"What is it?" she asked. "What are you doing?"

"The name is Lariquette," the man said as he absently traced the scratch marks on his cheek. "The time has come for you to make a decision, mademoiselle. You can be nice and convince me that you want to live, or else your life will end today."

Cassie stared in horror at the man. He was so callous, as if they were discussing what to prepare for breakfast. "Quanto promised me—"

"Quanto is no longer making the decisions," the Frenchman told her. "I'm the one who holds your fate in the palm of my hand." He paused to look her over slowly. "If you

137

want to live, you only have to show me a little consideration. That's not asking much.''

Even as Cassie was trying to think, the man took hold
of her wrist. He pulled her out of the tiny lean-to and into
the cabin. She managed to keep her feet under her, but there
was no strength in her legs. Fear paralyzed her muscles and
constricted her vocal cords. Her stomach rolled over and
became a great knot.

"You're pretty dirty from living in that hole," he said,
appraising her in the light. "Maybe you would like to take
a bath?''

"No, thank you.''

"You like being dirty? Is that it?''

Cassie did not reply. She stared at the hard-pack floor,
seeking strength or ideas.

"I remember when we grabbed you," Lariquette continued. "You were all ready to attend the Sunday meeting,
but I could tell you intended a lot more than that. You
wanted to impress the men in town, dazzle them with your
beauty." He snickered. "It was blatantly obvious.''

She held her silence.

"I've got a pan of heated water, there next to the fireplace." He continued to leer at her. "You can either wash
yourself, or maybe you would prefer I do it for you?''

Terror ripped a path across her inner chest. She felt panic
swell until it nearly overwhelmed her senses. It was all she
could do to give her head a negative shake.

"Am I to take that as a *no*?''

Cassie risked making eye contact. It confirmed her worst
fears. She could see what the man intended.

"If you touch me, Quanto will kill you," she managed
to say with some force. "You know he is a man of his
word.''

He gave a wave of his hand to dismiss her contention.

"Quanto is a smart man, but he's no match for me. The only reason I haven't killed him yet is so that he can take the blame for this whole affair. Once he shows with the money, he will have outlived his usefulness."

When Cassie had nothing to say to that, Lariquette stepped closer to her. She was again assailed by dread, but held her ground. To have any chance against the man, she would need some element of surprise. Quickly her eyes again flicked about, searching for some kind of weapon.

"We have an escape plan that is virtually foolproof, mademoiselle," he told her smoothly. "No one will ever catch us. Consider that a very good thing for you."

That caused her to pause. "For me?"

"No one will ever know what transpires between us," he whispered. "Do you not understand?"

She continued to stare at him.

"It is a simple bargain. You only have to be nice to me and I will let you live." He displayed a wicked smirk. "As no one will ever know, what could it hurt?" After a second, he cruelly added, "It isn't as if you have to protect your virtue. You're a widow, not a pure and innocent maiden."

The absurd logic penetrated through Cassie's fear. "I still have my honor, Mr. Lariquette. You cannot take that from me."

His expression clouded. "Think about your decision, mademoiselle. What good is your honor, if you are dead? I am offering you a trade—a few minutes of favor for your life!"

A surge of bitterness flooded through Cassie. She glared at him and hissed, "Not for a few minutes of favor, not even for one single touch! The price would be too high!"

She was not ready for the angry response. The Frenchman gave her a violent shove. She backpedaled into the wall, striking it hard enough that it knocked the wind out of her lungs.

"You stubborn little fool!" he snapped. "I'm offering you a chance to save your life! Don't you understand?"

Cassie remained pressed up against the wooden slabs. She ducked her head, as if cowed by his anger, while gathering both her breath and wits. There was nothing close at hand for her defense. She knew she was no match for the man's strength, but she would never submit. If he attacked her, she was going to fight back with all of her might. Her devotion belonged to John Fairbourn. With his image in her heart and mind, she would die before she would dishonor their love.

The door opened suddenly, and a lanky, rather skinny man entered the cabin.

Lariquette glared at the intrusion. "What are you doing, Cracker? I told you to stay out of the house!"

"Someone is coming!"

"You're dreaming! Quanto couldn't make it back here this early!"

"He might have exaggerated, just to keep us honest. I tell you, I can see a rider coming up from the south, maybe a half mile off."

Lariquette frowned. "From the south? Then it can't be Quanto. Get out there and keep watch!"

"You think it's a scout for a posse?" Cracker asked, his face showing a naked fear. "Maybe we ought to make a run for it."

"Don't turn yellow on me," the Frenchman said, growling. "If there's only one man, we'll grab him and see what's going on. It might even be a lone traveler, someone passing through."

"Not here. You remember what Quanto told us. No one ever comes up this way."

"Just do as I say!"

Cracker flinched, as if he had been slapped. "Sure, Frenchy, you're the boss."

He was no more than out the door, before Lariquette pointed at the hutch. "Back into your hole, mademoiselle, and"—he showed his teeth in a sneer—"if you know what's good for you, you'll keep your mouth shut."

Cassie didn't hesitate. She quickly ducked back into the hutch. When the door grated shut, she hurried over to look through the cracks in the walls. Was it John? Had he managed to find her somehow?

Being at the rear of the shack, she could see nothing but the interior of the cabin. She waited, anxious, her heart pounding with anticipation. With a humble reverence, she clasped her hands together and began to pray.

Luke was within a hundred yards when he spied the hovel, a wood and sod hut that had been built in the hollow between three hills. He instantly turned for the nearest cover, a small gully that bellied out from between two hills. It was not going to offer much protection, but it would hide his mount from sight.

He climbed down, secured his horse to a scraggly cedar, and pulled his rifle from the scabbard. Quickly, and as quietly as possible, he jacked a round into the chamber. Then he eased up the hill and crouched down behind a scraggly sage. For a moment, he surveyed the area and listened intently for anyone's approach.

Luke considered the numerous dilemmas. He had come upon the shack suddenly, unaware of its existence. If there was a guard, would they have seen his approach? Were the kidnappers even at this location? If so, was Cassie with them, or was she in transit somewhere for an exchange? He couldn't charge the cabin like an enraged bull, nor could he simply sit and wait. The money would have reached Broken Spoke yesterday or by early this morning. Quanto would want to leave them as little chance for preparation as possible, so he would have timed the exchange to coincide with the delivery of the money. There was a good chance the trade might have already taken place. He might be sneaking up on an empty cabin.

Beginning to move, he decided to have a look around. If there were a couple of horses in a corral or picketed where they could feed, he would at least know there was someone at the shack.

Holding the rifle between his hands, he made his way stealthily up the wash. The gentle slope of the hill was both a defense and an obstacle. Although it hid his movements, he could not see what was on the other side. Luke took his time, maneuvering up from sagebrush to clumps of wild grass, always keeping cover close at hand. As he neared the top of the rise, he kept his eyes trained on the summit, listening for anything out of the ordinary. Even as he approached the crest, he heard the footsteps!

Luke went onto his hands and knees and scooted over to a stand of dried grass. By stretching out on his back, he was able to conceal his position while still keeping his rifle ready for immediate use. He held his breath and waited.

A man's hat became visible first. After a moment, a head lifted higher, like a prairie dog rising warily from its hole. The man took a long look, but he was not far enough over the crest to see Luke's horse. There was a hesitation for a few seconds, then he came skulking over the top of the hill. He had a rifle between his hands, his eyes searching down the slope. A few steps led him past where Luke was hiding. When the man spotted Luke's horse, he displayed an alarmed look and scrambled to an outcrop of rocks for cover.

His position was on an even keel with Luke, but by ducking down, he was out of sight. Luke decided that a shot would alert anyone else at the cabin. He slipped his rifle over to one side and very slowly worked his body into a crouch. When he heard the crunch of the other man's boots, from taking a step, he rose up and charged the position. Three steps, then he sprang into a headlong lunge.

He caught the man concentrating down the hill. By the time he realized that Luke was coming at him, he didn't have time to turn the rifle and fire. He tried to spin to meet the attack, but Luke's body slammed into him. Both of them went down in a tangle, rolling and sliding down the hill together.

The man's rifle went flying, as the two of them grappled and fought for position. It was an awkward match, with both of them skidding and tumbling on the hillside. Luke got in a blow to the man's face, but was hit about the same time in the jaw. They flailed at one another between the tumbling and slipping on the incline.

The thin man might have been as good in a fight as Luke, but he had no confidence in himself. After a short slide, they both dug in enough to stop their descent down the hill. The other man tried to pull the pistol from his holster. The lowering of his guard allowed Luke a clear shot at his head. He launched a powerful punch, but slipped enough that his fist pounded his opponent right in the Adam's apple. It did more damage than a more solid hit to his jaw.

Gagging for air, the man dropped to his knees. He gasped while holding his throat with both hands. Luke could have smashed him into an unconscious heap, but chose to step back and pull his own pistol. He had the man covered while he slowly recovered.

"You're the escaped prisoner called Cracker," Luke deduced.

The thin man swallowed gingerly, still rubbing his throat. "You got a lucky punch in there, fella."

"Who is up at the cabin?"

"That's for me to know, stranger. Who are you?"

"Name's Mallory. I'm from Broken Spoke."

"Now what?"

"Depends on you, Cracker," Luke told him. "You can lend a hand, or I can kill you where you sit."

The man's face worked. He was not brave enough to laugh at the threat. "You fire the gun and there goes any chance of surprise. Frenchy will kill that gal, sure as you got the drop on me."

"Lariquette?"

"He's as cold-blooded as a snake, Mallory." Cracker began to feel some confidence. "He won't let you get within a rock toss of the cabin. He'll kill that girl before you can rescue her."

"Where's he at?"

"Liable to come over the top of the hill at any moment. He is better at this hunting game than me."

"What about Quanto?"

"Gone to pick up the ransom money. He'll be back at any time too. You don't have a chance against the two of them."

Luke did some quick thinking. The only prospect he had for getting past Lariquette was to let himself be taken prisoner. Otherwise, the man might panic and use Cassie as a shield. He might even kill her out of spite.

"You're a thief, Cracker," he said, trying a different approach. "What are you doing getting mixed up with a kidnapping and maybe murder?"

"Where could I have gone?" the man whined. "Quanto said he had a plan for getting us some money. We were only supposed to rob the old man at the ranch. Then there isn't but a little money in the safe. Lariquette and he decided to take the woman and trade her for ransom.'' He lowered his head sadly. ''I would never have done anything like that on my own. It wasn't my idea to kidnap the girl. I was against it from the first.''

''You'll hang for it all the same.''

Cracker licked his lips nervously, his eyes beading at the fearful prediction. ''I never wanted no part in it, Mallory! It ain't my fault. Those other two dragged me into this mess.''

''Maybe I can do something about that.''

Cracker's eyes widened. ''You can?''

''If you were to lend a hand getting Mrs. Hytower back, the court would surely look upon that favorably.''

''Like life in prison instead of hanging. Thanks a heap, Mallory.''

''Aiding in the rescue would be worth a lot. It might even get the charges against you dismissed.'' Luke watched for the man's reaction. ''You would still have to finish your original sentence, but if I vouched for you, I'll bet the judge would allow that your help was enough to offset any other crimes.''

Cracker did some hard thinking. ''I don't know, Mallory, Lariquette won't be an easy man to get the best of. He's about as crafty as a fox.''

''He might slip up, if we handle this right.''

''And how do we handle it right?''

Chapter Eighteen

Quanto had wasted no time. He was reasonably certain John would come alone. Between his affection for Cassandra and his own honor, he wasn't likely to attempt any trickery. Still, he had watched him for a few minutes to make doubly certain no one was following or lurking nearby for a signal.

He had stayed out of sight and waited until John left the satchel and rode off to get the directions for finding the girl. Once he was confident John was gone, Quanto had ridden down and picked up the money. It was all there, fifty thousand dollars!

He smiled to himself, keeping up a rapid pace toward the cabin. His plan was working to perfection. They would have no less than a three- or four-hour headstart. That meant they would reach the first station to the northwest well ahead of any posse. Once they changed for fresh horses, it would be another sixty miles due west to the next fresh mounts. Then a wide circle would bring them to the railroad. By the time a posse realized that they were bound for the Union Pacific, it would be too late. They would have gotten off a hundred miles down the track and be gone for good.

He should have been satisfied that everything about his ransom plan was going smoothly. However, he was plagued by a different uncertainty. His first concern was to make sure Cassandra was safe and secure. He had given her his promise, and she had given her own in return. He would let no harm come to her. Once he and the others were en route to their escape, she would only have to wait for John to arrive.

Quanto felt a churning within his chest at the thought. He visualized her running into the man's arms. They would cling to one another, lost lovers reunited. There would be an exchange of tender words, a vow of devotion, and possibly a thanks to God that they were safely back together.

In a moment of weakness, Quanto pondered how it would be to trade places with John. How pleasing it would be to enjoy the warmth of such a woman's embrace. To see love in her eyes, rather than terror; to hear a warm fondness in her voice, rather than have it quaking with fear; it would be reason enough to die for.

He shook the romantic nonsense from his brain. He had to stay alert. This was the most dangerous time since the kidnapping. If John or the others had any plan or trick card, it would be played now. He also had the Frenchman to worry about. A man who would kill an innocent girl to make a point was someone on whom he dared not turn his back. He would have to maintain a watchful eye on Lariquette until they parted company. The merciless killer was no more trustworthy than a bad-tempered rattlesnake.

He rode his animal hard, confident it wouldn't be needed

later. The horse under him was the one they would leave behind, because Cassandra would not be going with them. Exhausting the mount was of no consequence. There were still three fresh horses waiting at the hideout. Nothing could prevent their clean getaway to this point.

Keeping up the brisk gait, he did not slow down until he was within a quarter mile or so of the cabin. Then caution beckoned and he altered his course and pace. He circled to make his approach from a direction the other two men would not expect. Moving with the stealth of a hunter, he angled along the side of a small hillock and advanced to a short distance from the hidden cabin. His instincts warned him not to expose himself or ride over the top of a ridge and skyline himself. He was not about to make himself an easy target.

The prudence might have been an irrational concern, even a wasted exercise. Lariquette might indeed have a plan to be rid of him, but he would want to be sure Quanto had brought the money with him first. It would do him little good to kill Quanto and then find out something had gone amiss. If there had been a hitch, there might be no money, or Quanto could have taken the precaution of stashing the ransom before returning to the shack.

Skirting the lower rim of the hill, the small glen opened up before him. He took in the cabin and yard, the picketed horses, then suddenly jerked his horse to a stop. He stared open-mouthed at the scene before him, unable to believe his eyes.

Cracker was behind Luke Mallory, herding him along, with a rifle pointed at his back! Somehow, the man from Broken Spoke had found the hideout. Quanto about started forward, but there was a strange feel about the whole scene. Mallory had his hands behind him and was being escorted up toward the front of the cabin. But something was amiss.

A closer look revealed that Cracker was a full two steps back of Mallory and there was something in the prisoner's hand—a pistol!

"The rifle is empty!" Quanto guessed aloud. "Mallory is the one with the loaded gun!"

Lariquette appeared at the door. He had his six-shooter out, but relaxed at seeing Mallory was a prisoner, and by now Mallory's gun was hidden. Quanto knew what to expect. Without hesitation, he turned his horse back away from the old shack, remaining out of sight.

Luke watched for the Frenchman to lower his guard. He could see a couple of recent scratches on the man's face. He feared it was evidence of his struggle with Cassie. An inner rage churned and knotted in his chest. If she had been harmed, he would see that all three of these vermin paid the ultimate price. First, he had to get the drop on both men. His main worry was Cracker. If he lost his resolve and gave Lariquette a warning, Luke might be too slow getting his gun into play.

"You got him," Lariquette commended the skinny man. "Good for you."

"What do we do with him?" Cracker asked.

Luke moved to within a step of the cabin, watching for an opening. A smugness showed on Lariquette's face. He was overconfident now.

"What else?" the man replied, waving his gun hand. "We kill him."

The direction of his gun was diverted away from Luke as he motioned with it. It was the opening needed. Luke quickly jerked his gun out of hiding and covered Lariquette.

"Think again, you murdering scum!"

The Frenchman was stunned. He froze in position, gun

still in his grasp, but with no chance of shooting Luke before being shot himself. He paused to put an accusing look on Cracker.

"He had the drop on me!" the scrawny man quickly explained. "The rifle is empty! I couldn't do nothing!"

"Drop the gun!" Luke ordered, taking a step back, but keeping his pistol aligned with Lariquette's chest. "Do it!"

The man's face contorted into a mask of fury. With a sneer of contempt, he finally threw his gun to the ground. "You yella' coward, Cracker! I could have gut-shot him on the spot! All you had to do was give me the nod!"

"I couldn't risk it, Frenchy! He'd have killed me for sure!"

Luke stepped off to one side and turned enough to catch sight of the gaunt man from the corner of his eye. "Now you, Cracker! Let's go!"

He tossed his rifle into the dirt and lifted his hands up as high as if he was trying to pick stars out of the sky. He didn't walk, but did a rapid tiptoe over next to Lariquette. All the while, he was shaking his head woefully. "I didn't have no choice," he repeated. "It ain't my fault."

"Cracker, where is some rope?" Luke asked. "I want you both tied up before Quanto arrives."

"It's a little late for that, Mallory," a cutting voice came from behind Luke. "You even twitch and you're dead!"

Quanto was at the corner of the cabin, a rifle trained squarely on Luke's chest. Luke ventured a glance that way, but realized any attempt to spin and fire would be wasted. A bullet to his heart was only a split second away. He put an accusing look on Cracker, but he could see the fear shining in his eyes. He hadn't expected Quanto back yet.

"Don't even think about trying your luck," Quanto warned. "I killed Preston Hytower, and he didn't even have a gun."

"Maybe you'll kill me all the same, whether I give up or not."

"Maybe."

Luke held his pistol tightly for a full second, then let it drop from his hand. He had failed to rescue Cassie. Worse, he was now a captive himself.

"Shoot him!" Lariquette growled. "Kill the nosy coot and let's get out of here."

"The man is probably a sworn-in deputy marshal," Quanto told the Frenchman. "I don't want an army of lawmen on my tail. We got the money. That's what we've been after."

Lariquette retrieved his pistol and stared at Cracker. The thin man threw a hasty, nervous glance at Luke, then hurried over to pick up his rifle. Even as he reached for the gun, a blast rang out.

Luke staggered back a step, shocked, thinking he had been shot. But the bullet had been aimed at the slim, frightened little man.

The slug hit Cracker in the center of the chest. His eyes grew wide in horror, his mouth agape in surprise, then he flopped flat onto his back. In the following moment of complete silence, a ragged expulsion of his final breath was the only sound to be heard.

"What's the idea, Frenchy?" Quanto demanded, once he was sure the man was dead.

"He betrayed us!" Lariquette replied. "There's no reason why he couldn't have warned me about Mallory here having a gun. Any sign from Cracker at all and I would have known to kill him. The man was a double-crossing, craven coward."

"All right, but let's get out of here. There will be more men coming pretty soon. We need as much headstart as possible."

Lariquette still had his gun out, but Quanto had not lowered his own guard. Luke could see that neither of them trusted the other. He kept quiet and watched. If one of them turned to fire at the other, he would make a dive for his own gun.

"Still your show, Quanto," Lariquette said, holstering his weapon, as if the thought had never entered his mind. "What now?"

"Round up Mallory's horse, then saddle us the two best mounts. I'll tie up both this guy and the woman, and we'll leave them at the cabin. We'll take the horses down the trail apiece so Mallory can't follow. All we need is a few minutes' lead and no one will ever catch us."

"You're the boss."

Quanto herded Mallory into the cabin and dug out a piece of cord to tie his hands. "Turn around, get on your knees, and put your hands behind your back," he ordered. "Lariquette would just as soon kill you, so I suggest you do as I say."

"I kind of figured you would be wanting to see me dead too. After all, I was the one who helped catch and send you to jail. I'm also the one who brought along Tito, and he killed your partner, Yarrow."

"I've got my payback for all you done on my horse, fifty thousand apologies from John Fairbourn and Mont Hytower."

"I thought a lot of things about you, Quanto, but never figured you for a kidnapper."

"The woman hasn't been harmed. You keep your mouth shut and you won't be harmed either."

Luke had no choice. He knelt down on the hard-pack floor and offered no resistance. His life was in the hands of the half-breed.

Quanto bound his wrists, but he didn't seem too concerned about the knots. Because the kidnappers had taken the horses and had an escape route all planned, Luke and the girl offered no real threat to them.

"All right, into the hutch with the girl."

Luke did as he was told, ducking into the small lean-to. There was relief on Cassie's face at seeing him, yet a dread that he had been caught.

"You don't release him for five full minutes, Mrs. Hytower," Quanto told her. "Do you understand?"

"I do," she replied quietly.

"Your word?"

She hesitated only for a second. "Yes."

"Then I wish you a safe return to your home and John Fairbourn." He started to leave, but Cassie stopped him.

"Quanto?"

Luke turned around, facing the half-breed, so he could begin to work on the cords. He saw the man pause at the small doorway. There was an agonized look on his face, as if having the girl call him by his actual name caused him a great inner pain. "What?"

"Don't trust the Frenchman. I know he wants all of the money for himself, and he wants me dead, so I can never testify against him."

Luke twisted one hand and began to tug at the knots. He was nearly free of the rope.

"I'll watch him, Mrs. Hytower. Don't you worry about—"

"About me?" Lariquette had slipped back up to the cabin. He was at the entrance, his gun pointed at Quanto. A cruel smirk spread across his lips. "A little late for that."

"You're supposed to be getting the horses," Quanto said with a growl. "We don't have much time."

"I changed my mind," Lariquette retorted. "As of this

minute, I'm taking over. If you want to ride with me, that's fine. We can split the money two ways.''

''But?''

''But there will be no witnesses.''

Luke worked feverishly against the cords. Twisting and pulling, he felt the burning of the hide as the rope abraded the skin about his wrists. Time was short. A second, maybe two, and he would be faced with certain death. Quanto's gun was in his holster. He had no chance against the Frenchman. If Luke could get himself free, he might be able to jump Quanto and get his gun. The odds against him doing that, then being able to shoot Lariquette, without getting killed first, were slim at best. The alternative was certain death.

Quanto, however, moved to block the access to the hutch. ''We can get away without any trouble or any more killing, Frenchy. You know the plan.''

''I'm not going to spend my life looking over my shoulder or ducking into an alley at the sight of a badge. The only ties between you and me are that we escaped at the same time. Without anyone to point a finger at me, I can start out fresh. The manslaughter charge isn't enough to badger me for life, but kidnapping is a different story.''

''Murdering a woman is even worse, Frenchy.'' He narrowed his gaze. ''But then, you already know all about that, don't you? Mrs. Hytower wouldn't be the first woman you've killed.''

Lariquette cocked the pistol, his face a stone mask. ''Two choices, Quanto—come with me, or die with the lady and her pal.''

Quanto seemed aware of the fact that Luke was about free, even though his eyes never left the man at the doorway. He slowly lowered his hand to the butt of his gun.

"Guess this is where it ends, Frenchy. Either take the money and ride, or start shooting."

The Frenchman gave a slight lift to his shoulders and let them drop. His lips curled upward and he said, "Have it your way."

Even as the blast of the gun filled the room, the half-breed jerked his gun from its holster. The bullet hit him in the chest, and he backed up a step. Luke managed to pull his hands free as Lariquette fired twice more. Quanto was like a statue of granite. He held his ground, absorbing the bullets and preventing any chance for the Frenchman to get a clear shot at Luke or the girl. With the last possible strength in his body, Quanto pitched his gun into the hutch.

Luke grabbed the pistol and tried to aim between the boards. He fired a hasty shot at the Frenchman, driving him back from the door. The bullet missed its target, but it was enough to send Lariquette scampering away. Luke might have run after him, but Quanto's legs finally gave out. He sagged downward. If not for Luke catching him, he would have crashed to the floor.

"Quanto!" Cassie was quickly at the man's side. She helped Luke lay the man down and pulled back a hand that was covered with blood. "Oh, dear!" she gasped. "He's hurt bad."

The sound of a horse racing from the yard told of the Frenchman's escape. Luke could not go after him, not while Quanto was dying in his arms. The man had forfeited his life to protect him and the girl.

Cassie was busy opening Quanto's shirt, trying desperately to stop the bleeding. It took only a glance for Luke to see the effort was wasted. Any one of the three bullets looked to be fatal.

"I'm sorry, Quanto," Cassie whispered. "I'm so sorry."

But Quanto rolled his head back and forth in a negative

motion. "I . . . I promised you that I wouldn't let any harm come to you." He set his teeth against the pain. "I kept my word."

"Yes," Cassie murmured. "You kept your word."

Quanto diverted his stare to Luke. "You tell Fairbourn he's a . . ." He coughed and grimaced from the searing agony. "Tell him he's a lucky man."

"I'll tell him."

With a heavy sigh, Quanto closed his eyes, allowing the reaper of death to take him away.

Chapter Nineteen

Joe had sent the Ingersol brothers to either side of the trail. They had heard a lone shot some minutes earlier. Now several more. He didn't know what it meant, but he was smart enough to approach with caution.

"I see him!" Don called. "One rider!"

"Yeah," Ray joined in. "Coming this way!"

Joe pulled his rifle and jacked a shell into the chamber. He could see the man as well, the horse racing as if its tail were on fire. He worried that Luke might have run into the three kidnappers and tried to take them on alone.

"Is it one of them?" Don asked.

"The gambler, Lariquette," Joe told him, recalling the description. "He won't want to come without a fight."

The three of them rode an intercept course and pulled up fifty yards in front of the charging rider. Lariquette had been so busy looking over his shoulder that he didn't see the three of them waiting. He was nearly in the midst before he yanked the horse to one side.

"Hold it!" Ray called out. "We're the law!"

The Frenchman jerked his pistol and fired a hasty shot in their direction. Before Joe could give the order, Don leveled his rifle and pulled the trigger.

Lariquette rocked forward in the saddle, then toppled off the back of his horse. He landed grotesquely on his head and shoulders and flopped over onto his face. The horse shied off a short distance and slowed to a stop.

"Good shot," Joe told Don.

"Donny is a holy terror with a rifle," Ray observed. "Don't remember the last time he took more than one shot to drop a deer or antelope, not even at a full run."

"He's done," Don added. "I put the slug right through his brisket."

Casting ordinary caution aside, Joe rode over to the body. He concluded that Don was right. Having witnessed a fair number of men drop during a fight, he was reasonably certain Lariquette would not be getting back up.

"He's our man," he announced, drawing close enough to see the man's face. "And I see a couple fresh scratches on his cheek."

"Could be from the hostage or when he might have killed the Kensington girl," Don suggested. He had followed Joe to look over the body.

Joe looked off toward the small valley ahead. "I'd say the shooting we heard came from over the next hill."

"Wonder where the other two are?" Don asked.

"We got the right one," Ray announced from a few feet away.

They both looked over to see him holding the reins to Lariquette's horse. He had the satchel open between his hands. "Dad blame! I never seen so much money in all my life!"

"If the girl is okay, you'll get your bonus," Joe said, wondering if he could trust the two brothers with so much money.

However, Ray didn't show any sign of becoming greedy. "We best go have us a look," he said, securing the satchel back onto Lariquette's horse. He mounted up and led the animal over to the dead body.

"You don't think the shots we heard was this here gent killing his partners and . . ." Don stopped speaking. "Geez, I hope we're not too late."

After tossing the body over the horse, the three men hurried along the trail. As the cabin came into view, Joe spied another corpse lying in the yard.

"Don't look good," Ray said. "Is that Quanto or the thief?"

"Cracker would be my guess," Joe said, identifying the slender form. "He was tall and skinny."

"Ah, no," Don said and groaned. "We're too late. The girl is going to be—"

But his words were cut short. As they entered the yard, Luke came out of the building. He raised a hand in greeting, a smile of relief on his face. It took only a glance to know that Lariquette had not made good his escape.

"Glad to see you in one piece," Joe said. "How about the young lady?"

"Inside. She's okay."

"Whew!" Don let out a deep sigh. "When we caught this guy heading for places unknown, we figured he had done everyone else in."

"He would have, if not for Quanto. He gave his life to save ours."

"Doesn't sound like the act of a kidnapper," Ray said.

"Looks like we get a bonus," Don said to change the subject. "We got the money back, the girl, and all three kidnappers."

Luke gave a nod of his head. "I think you can count on Mont being generous, fellows. This worked out just fine."

Cracker and Quanto were each draped over the backs of their horses, standing alongside that of Lariquette, when John Fairbourn arrived. Luke walked over to meet him and gave his lathered mount the once-over.

"Dad gum, Fairbourn! You about killed this poor animal. You would have taken a belt to Billy, if he had been so hard on a horse."

John didn't answer, but glanced quickly around the yard. His search ended when he found Cassie, standing at the doorway. Without a word, he jumped down to the ground. Cassie bolted forward, crossing the distance at a run, and plunged into his arms. The force of catching her about caused him to lose his balance, but he recovered at once to wrap her within his arms. She wept against his chest from the pent-up emotions and relief.

"Funny," Luke teased, "she didn't greet me with such affection."

John held Cassie for a few long moments, until she recouped her aplomb. When she stepped back, he gave her a short appraisal. "What a beautiful sight," he said softly.

Cassie managed a smile. She was dirty from being kept in a damp hovel and sleeping on the ground, her eyes were red, cheeks tear-streaked, with a smudge on one side of her face, and her hair tangled and stringy. "I think you had better have your eyes checked, Mr. Fairbourn. You are surely going blind."

"Blinded by your radiance," he returned smoothly.

"Missed a little excitement, John," Luke said, butting in.

John paused to take notice of the three bodies. "Looks like you got them all."

"Joe and the Ingersol boys bagged Lariquette. As for the other two, Lariquette was the one who killed them both."

Joe had moved close enough that he could hear their words. He hooked a thumb back to the younger Ingersol. "Don was the one who nailed him. The boy is a good shot."

"Quanto saved both Mr. Mallory and myself," Cassie explained. "If he hadn't kept his word, the Frenchman would have killed us as well."

"She's right on that count, John. Quanto took three slugs and still managed to toss me his gun. I reckon the breed had some good in him after all."

"We think one of these men killed Sally Kensington," John informed them. "I can't imagine Quanto giving up his life for you two and being involved in something like that."

"It must have been the Frenchman," Cassie determined. "I was blindfolded, but I know he left us at the creek and didn't return for a couple days. Plus, once Quanto was gone to collect the ransom, he allowed me to see him. There were some scratch marks on his face."

"Reckon he's the one," Luke said gravely. "I'm real sorry about Sally. She was a real sweet kid."

"He murdered some innocent girl to prove they were serious?" the Indian asked.

Luke paused to introduce Joe to Cassie. He gave her a polite nod, but held out a couple slips of paper for Luke to see. "Found these two receipts on Lariquette. Looks like he bought some horses."

"Lucky you got here in time to intercept him, Joe. If

he'd gotten a good jump on us, we might never have caught up with him. With a change of horses stashed in a couple different places, they must have had quite an escape plan."

"I overheard them talking about it once," Cassie put in. "The plan was to arrange for a change of horses twice, each about sixty miles apart. Then they were going to take the train and get off at Evanston."

"If they let you hear all that, it's no wonder they were going to kill you."

"The Frenchman intended to kill me all along. I could see it in his eyes."

Joe rubbed his chin thoughtfully. "You mentioned that Lariquette was gone for a couple days. When did he return?"

"Yesterday morning."

"That would fit," John said. "Dexter found Sally yesterday. It appears she was killed during the previous night."

"So they planned to take us sixty miles in one direction, swap horses, go another sixty miles, then swap again?"

"I think so."

Joe continued to frown. "If you've no objections, paleface, I'll go see if I can round up those horses. They are sitting and waiting to be claimed, and I have the bill of sale for them."

"I imagine Mont will pay you for your trouble. After all, the horses were bought with his money."

Joe left them without another word, mounted up, and rode off in a southwesterly direction. The two Ingersol boys were also on their horses, waiting patiently.

"We'll have to take it easy," John said. "I about ran my horse to death getting here."

"It appears Quanto only wanted a couple hours' head-start."

''The strategy gave him as much time as he needed. He probably only watched long enough to make certain I was alone. Then I had to ride in the opposite direction to find the note telling of this cabin's location. By the time I could have summoned any help, they would have had another hour or more. With their escape plan so neatly laid out, we would never have overtaken them.''

''You up to a ride?'' Luke asked Cassie.

''For a hot bath and clean clothes, I would walk barefoot all the way home.''

''I'd say that qualifies as a yes,'' John said.

Luke waited until everyone was ready, then, taking the reins of the horse carrying Lariquette's body, he led the way. Each of the Ingersol boys had a horse in tow, with John and Cassie bringing up the rear. It was an easy five or six hours to Broken Spoke. Having to stop and rest several times, they would be lucky to beat the darkness.

Chapter Twenty

Amber picked up a few pieces of wood for the stove. She paused to look under the log, where she had witnessed Leland hiding his treasure. She had barely tucked it into her pocket when she heard a horse coming along the trail. She hurried to the front of the house in time to meet Cully Deeks.

He pulled his mount to a stop and smiled. Turning sideways, he hooked one leg up over the pommel and relaxed.

"Well, my luck is getting better," he said in greeting her. "I was afraid I would have to ask your mother where you were at. You being outside here saved me the chore."

"What do you want?"

Cully was taken aback at the cool retort. "I expect you know the answer to that."

"You came to visit me?"

"The monthly dance is this Saturday night. I was hoping you would let me escort you to and from. Big George offered me the use of his calash. It's cozy for two, as nice a buggy as you'll find in the valley.''

''What about Mrs. Hytower? Any word yet?''

''No, ma'am. But we should hear something by later tonight or first thing in the morning.''

''And this dance is going to be held, no matter what has happened?''

''I expect so. There ain't been one of these affairs canceled in more'n a year.''

''It won't be real festive, if the kidnappers are still at large and something bad has happened.''

''I aim to keep a categorical conviction about it all, Miss Amber. Everything is going to turn out fine.''

''Why did you choose me?''

''My two best friends are John Fairbourn and Luke Mallory. They both have real pretty gals to swing about the dance floor with.'' He showed his easy smile. ''I would be real proud to have you on my arm. Might say, it would put me on an even keel with them.''

Amber was torn inside. The anxiety and suspicions caused a never-ending ache in her stomach and had robbed her of a decent night's sleep. She hated the way she felt about Leland. On the other hand, she was quite taken with Cully Deeks. There was something about him that stirred her heart and whose presence filled her with a lightness, a wondrous sort of energy. It seemed she always felt a little giddy and was filled with cheer whenever he had come around. She finally summoned a teasing smile. ''Would you like to speak to my mother?''

The courage appeared to have deserted Cully. He hesitantly looked at the house and back to Amber. ''Do I have to?''

''Do you want to take me to the dance or not?''

"I thought I would only have to ask your oldest brother, Ray. He's kind of the man about the house, ain't he?"

"Yes, but you recall that he is part of the special posse. He isn't home." She narrowed her gaze. "You're not afraid of my ma, are you?"

"She seems a formidable woman."

Amber laughed. "All right, you big chicken, I'll tell her I'm going with you to the dance. Is that better?"

A wide smile came into his face. "Yes, ma'am."

"Well, you better get out of here. If she comes out to see what is going on, you'll have to buck up and ask her face-to-face."

Cully swung his leg back and found the stirrup with his foot. He paused to reach up and touch the brim of his hat. "I'm thanking you again, Miss Amber. I'll see you on Saturday night, about sunset."

He had not ridden a hundred yards before Edna came out the door. It was obvious that she had heard every word.

"Since when don't you ask my permission, before you go telling a man how you're going to a shindig with him?"

"We had already talked about it some, Ma."

She snorted. "Well, guess you ain't no child anymore."

"No, Ma."

Edna put a curious look on her. "And I've been real concerned about the way you been moping about lately. Has it all been because of this here Deeks fella?"

"No, Ma," she answered. "There has been other things on my mind."

"Well, things is changed now. Everything is going to come up roses." Edna showed a rare smile. "With the money the boys are going to make on that there posse, we're going to buy enough supplies to get us by until they can find work."

"That'll be fine."

"So why the long face? I'd think you would be bubbling over with anticipation!"

Amber sighed deeply and fished into her skirt pocket. "There's something I got to show you, Ma," She pulled out a square piece of white material, as smooth as a baby's cheek, except for a little stitching in one corner.

Edna took the cloth from her and examined it closely. It was a white handkerchief with a name monogrammed on it. "Where did you get this?"

"I seen Leland hide it in the woodpile. He was real nervous when I come by."

A mist came into Edna's eyes. She blinked it away at once. "It might not mean nothing, girl. He could have found it."

"He's been acting real strange of late. You know he ain't even had no appetite."

"Ray's been gone," Edna said defending him. "The boy worships Ray."

"Yeah, Ma, but . . ." Amber ducked her head. "What if he done something bad?"

Edna handed back the piece of material. "Didn't you hear the news in town? The kidnappers killed the Kensington girl to show everyone they were serious."

"You think that's what happened? Leland maybe come onto Sally after she was dead and took this?"

"He might have just picked it up. He could have found it on the ground, where the girl was attacked. The story is, the killer carried her up near the road, where she was sure to be seen. That sure makes sense for the kidnappers, but not for anyone else."

"I guess you're right."

"Here, you put this back where you got it from. I'll speak to Leland when . . ."

168 *Terrell L. Bowers*

Amber took a step, then stopped at the pause in her mother's sentence.

"It's the boys!" Edna exclaimed happily. "They's back!"

Ray and Don arrived with shouts and war whoops. Amber and Edna hurried over to greet them. Leland must have seen them from where he had been mending the corral fence. He waved his arms and hollered back, obviously ecstatic to see his brothers again.

"Whatta' you think, Ma," Ray called out, "Donny nailed the one what was getting away. Downed him with a single shot."

"That's my boy!" Edna praised him. "You get the girl back too?"

"She's right as spring rain," Ray replied, pulling up at the front of the house. He grinned at his brother. "How you been doing here alone, Leland? You been taking good care of Ma and Amber?"

"Ah-yeah!" He was jovial, even gleeful about having Ray back. "Ah-yeah! I been taking good care of them."

The boys dismounted and Ray reached into his pocket and pulled out some paper money. "We're sitting high on the fence now, Ma. Old man Hytower give us each a year's pay as bonus for getting the gal back safely."

"What's that?"

"Yep." He was all smiles. "Five hundred dollars each! Can you imagine that?"

Edna shook her head in wonder. "We ain't never had that much money, not even from selling the house when your pa died."

"Everything is going to be sweet as fudge from now on." He continued his jubilation. "With this money, we can turn in these borrowed nags and buy us some real horses. We'll be able to get the farm equipment we need and add onto the house. We're on top of the world.''

''Sounds like you've got all the money spent already!'' Donny complained. ''I was wanting to get me a new rifle.''

''Don't get your hat on crossways, kid, we might work it into the budget.''

''We got us a dog while you was gone,'' Leland told Ray. ''He likes me real good. He comes when I call him and everything.''

''Did you give him a name yet?''

''I been calling him Pepper, Ray. He likes when I call him that.''

''Pepper it is.'' He reached out and patted Leland on the shoulder. ''I like it!''

''Ah-yeah! He's a good dog.''

''First thing in the morning, we're going to town and buy us everything we need.'' Ray looked over at Amber. ''Bet you could use a new dress, being that you are going to a dance and all.''

''What makes you think that?''

''Passed that cow tender up the trail a ways. He was grinning like the only ram in a herd of sheep.''

Amber was suddenly self-conscious. ''I never thought . . .''

''We'll buy you the prettiest dress in Broken Spoke, Little Sister. What do you say?''

''We don't want to throw the money away,'' Edna said. However, she immediately showed a slight smile. ''But you're right about a new dress. Amber is entering the courting age. She will need to look pretty.''

Ray grew serious. ''Speaking of pretty, we heard about Sally Kensington. That's a real shame. Only met her the one time, but she was a cute kid.''

Edna was also somber. ''The guesswork is that them

kidnapper fellows done kilt her so everyone would know they was serious.''

"The guy Donny shot had some scratches on his face. Mrs. Hytower said he was not at the hideout for a couple days, so we figure it was him.''

"You say he had scratches on his face?'' Amber asked.

"Looked like nail marks on one cheek. They was a couple days old, so the timing was about right. Mallory also said that the half-breed accused the Frenchman of murdering a woman, except it didn't mean anything to him at the time.''

Amber exchanged looks with her mother. Edna gave a firm nod of her head and said pointedly, "I'm right glad you got him, Donny. Any man who would kill a helpless young girl don't deserve to live.''

"It's too late to go to town tonight,'' Ray said. "Hope there's some food in the house.''

"We got enough to get by till tomorrow,'' Edna replied.

Don chuckled. "Tomorrow, we'll buy out the store. Nothing but the best for us from here on out.''

There was laughing and joking all around. Even Amber began to feel the cloud lift. There was the explanation she needed. Quanto had accused Lariquette of killing Sally. He even had the scratches on his face from a woman's nails. If Mrs. Hytower had not been involved with the act, what other answer was there? Her fears about Leland were not founded. He had either found the silk handkerchief, or he had stumbled onto the body and taken it. His guilt at removing something from the girl would have been enough to cause him to be withdrawn and moody.

Regardless, Edna could handle it now. She would mention it to Ray and he would get the truth of the matter. Whichever way her brother had come to have possession of the hankie, there was no real harm done.

Chapter Twenty-one

Amber was self-conscious about attending the dance with Cully Deeks. She had never primped and fussed so much before in her life. After a bath, she washed her hair, then spent an hour tossing and fluffing to dry it, plus the better part of a second hour forcing it to curl the way she wanted it. The dress was pink, with lace at the collar and sleeves, with a matching lace flounce. The underskirt was of stiff material, enough to distend the dress outward and prevent it from simply hanging limply. She even endured the impediment of a crested-shaped bustle at the back of the skirt. A ribbon, matching the color of the dress, was used to hold the bulk of her hair in place, other than for the tediously formed ringlets next to each ear. She even had new shoes, which were bound to cause blisters before the night was over. A bit of rouge to add color to her cheeks and lips and she was ready an hour before there came the sound of an approaching buggy.

"It's him," Donny said, looking out the window. He turned back and looked over at Ray. "Think we ought to tag along?"

Ray had been quiet, ever since the return from town. Amber glanced at him, ready for his jest or tease. However, he didn't seem to have heard his brother.

"Ray?" Donny spoke up again. "You awake?"

He jumped, as if he had been off in a dreamland somewhere. "Yeah, yeah, I hear you."

"So?"

"So what?"

"Are we going to let that cow sitter escort Sis into town all by himself?"

"Wouldn't want him thinking he has a free hand to do whatever he wants," Ray answered. "We'll keep them company."

"You're too good to me," Amber complained.

"No one can say we don't watch you proper," Ray told her.

"I think Leland had best stay home with me," Edna jumped into the conversation. "I haven't been feeling real good this afternoon."

Donny was quick to look at her. "Why didn't you say something, Ma? We don't have to go to the silly dance."

"No, no." She waved a hand to dismiss his concern. "You boys and Amber go and have a good time. Leland can tend to my needs."

Ray stared at her with an odd expression. "Ma, I—"

"You do as I say, Raymond Ingersol."

The use of his full name was a warning. Whenever Edna used a proper title, it was time to walk a fine and straight line. He knew there would be no arguments.

The sound came of a carriage stopping and a moment

later there was a light tap at the door. Donny opened it at once.

Cully was in a clean suit of clothes, with polished boots and a new hat. Someone had done a fair job of trimming his hair and he had a smooth, freshly shaven face. In his hand was a tin of sweets.

"I 'spect you're here to court my sister?" Donny confronted him.

"I am," Cully said.

"What do you think, Leland?" Don asked as his brother came over from where he had been saddling horses for the three of them.

"I don't know, Donny," he answered. "What do I think?"

Amber walked over to stand back of Donny. "You boys quit hazing Mr. Deeks," she said. "He's trying to do this proper and you're scaring him to death."

"I reckon they ain't scaring me none, Miss Amber," Cully replied, flashing a nervous grin. "I surely aim to see this through."

She admired his courage and stepped forward, gently shoving Donny to one side. There was an instant warmth that spread through her at the way Cully's eyes lit up. He drank in her radiance from head to foot and let out a deep sigh.

"Man oh man! Ain't no one going to have a prettier girl on his arm than me tonight."

Amber felt a rush of heat come to her cheeks. She went quickly through the door, using the act of leaving to hide her embarrassment. "Let's get a move on, Mr. Deeks."

"We'll be right behind you," Donny teased.

"Ah-yeah!" Leland joined in. "We'll be right behind."

As Cully offered his hand to help Amber climb aboard the two-passenger carriage, Ray moved out and put a hand on Leland's shoulder. Even as she situated the full skirt and sat down, she glimpsed the disappointment enter her brother's face. Leland listened to what Ray whispered to him, nodding obediently.

"Come on into the house, Leland," Edna said from the porch. "I'm going to make a batch of brownies. You can have some while they're still hot from the oven."

Leland still had the long face, but he plodded over to the house. Pepper came up to him looking for affection. The big boy bent over to scratch the dog's ears, and watched with a forlorn expression while Ray and Donny went over and mounted up.

Cully picked up the reins, turned the buggy around, and prompted the horse to move down the road at an easy trot. Amber felt a pang of sympathy for Leland, but thoughts of him were quickly pushed from her mind. She wrung her hands together, apprehensive at the prospect of dancing close to a man. With no coaching on the etiquette of courtship, she was uncertain as to how to behave. She had danced with Donny and Ray a time or two, but this was going to be a whole new experience for her.

"I hope you'll allow for my awkwardness, Miss Amber," Cully said after a moment. "I've never really done much of this courting. I don't rightly know all the rules."

She replied that the admission about made them even, but instead, she felt relieved. "I won't be hesitant about letting you know if you make any mistakes, Mr. Deeks."

He chuckled. "I wouldn't want to get my face slapped."

Allowing a simper to play on her lips, she regarded him with her own mischievous eyes. "Then you best mind your manners. With Ray and Donny looking over our shoulders, I don't think a slap is the worst thing you have to fear."

"I intend to be the perfect gentleman, Miss Amber. Yes, ma'am, the perfect gentleman."

*   *   *

The guitar player and two fiddlers were taking a break from playing, so most people were milling about, chatting or lined up at the refreshment table. Luke was holding Timony's hand when he saw Joe stick his head into the room. The Indian gave a nod, indicating he would wait outside.

"Looks like Joe made it back," he said. "You want to get us a drink while I see what he's up to?"

"If you promise not to go galavanting off on the trail of more kidnappers or killers."

"That ought to be a safe promise," he agreed, reluctantly letting go of her hand.

Joe was standing a few feet away from the Ace High entrance. There was a look of concern etched into his face.

"What say, Joe? You get the horses back all right?"

"Dropped them off at the Hytower place. Mont paid me and offered a job too."

"Reckon you could do worse. Mont would be a good man to work for. He needs a foreman to manage his place."

"A few Hereford bulls and a small remuda of horses? Wouldn't exactly be a lot to keep a man busy."

"Give you time to start that newspaper."

Joe seemed to only half hear the words. "I've a special reason for stopping by, paleface." He appeared to struggle with the next words. "Who did you say did the investigative work on the murder of that young girl?"

"Cully Deeks."

"Best call him over for a minute."

Luke frowned, but Joe was not going to repeat whatever he had in mind. Returning to the door, he spied Cully, standing with the Ingersol girl. He caught his eye and motioned him over.

"What do you want, Mallory?"

"Joe has a couple questions for you."

"I'll be right back," Cully told Amber.

"Is this something my delicate ears can't listen to?"

"I don't know."

"Then I'll go with you. I've never heard an Indian speak before."

"He's not your ordinary Indian, ma'am," Luke warned her.

As she seemed determined to come along, Cully did not object. Luke didn't know what to expect, but decided the girl was on her own. He led the way over to where Joe was standing.

"All right, Joe, here's Cully Deeks. The lady is Amber Ingersol."

Joe nodded at Deeks, but ignored Amber.

Cully grinned. "Heard you did a bang-up job catching those kidnappers, Joe. Glad you also solved our murder case."

Joe sighed. "I don't believe Lariquette was responsible for the murder of the girl here in Broken Spoke."

Luke was speechless, numbed by the deduction. Cully was also at a loss for words. Oddly, it was Amber who was first to speak.

"Why do you say that?"

"The problem is the time of the murder," Joe went on. "Am I correct in assuming the girl was killed sometime Tuesday night or early Wednesday morning?"

"Dexter Cline found her body about noon on Wednesday. Sally left the house Tuesday afternoon or early evening, so that's right."

Joe pulled a piece of paper from his pocket. "I have here the two bills of sale, one is from the town of Sherman, where Lariquette purchased three horses on Monday. The second is dated Tuesday, over at Cameron Flats, where the Frenchman had stabled the horses. Cameron Flats is no less than sixty miles away. I find it difficult to imagine him being able to return here, kill the girl, then get all the way back to the cabin hideout by Wednesday morning. You recall Mrs. Hytower said Lariquette returned on Wednesday morning.''

Luke shook his head. ''Quanto as much as accused the Frenchman of the murder, but Lariquette didn't say anything back. It was the heat of the moment, right before the shooting started.''

''And you're sure that Quanto wouldn't have killed the girl?''

''Mrs. Hytower said he treated her very decently. She seemed positive he wouldn't have done anything to harm Sally.''

''Then we still have a killer running loose.''

''What's going on?'' a voice came from the darkness. All of them turned to see Ray approach.

''The Frenchman didn't kill the Kensington girl, Ray,'' Amber told him. ''It was physically impossible for him to have been in the area at the time.''

Ray should have looked surprised, but he didn't. Instead, a flood of anguish swept over his features and he lowered his head.

''Looks like we're back where we started,'' Cully said. ''Maybe Joe here can find a clue as to who did the killing. I didn't find anything but a single footprint.''

''Ray?'' Amber spoke up. ''Is there something we should know?''

Luke wondered what the girl was referring to. Her brother appeared to choke up, as if there were words trying to escape, but he couldn't speak.

Amber reached out and placed her hand on Ray's shoulder. In a very gentle voice, she asked, ''Was it Leland?''

The man took a deep breath and let it out slowly. When

he looked at the waiting group, there were tears in his eyes. He slowly shook his head back and forth.

"Sally toyed with me and my brother the first time we met Tom. She kind of gave us the eye and smiled, you know, just being coy." He had to pause to swallow, struggling against the lump in his throat. "Leland said he ran into her at the creek while he was fishing. She was about to wade across and take the shortcut into town. He . . ." Ray stopped, as his voice cracked from the strain. "He didn't mean to hurt her. He only wanted to have a story for me when we got back. He wanted to tell me how he had kissed a girl. He thought how I would brag on him for being such a ladies' man."

"But Sally wouldn't let him, is that it?" Cully asked.

"He said how, when he caught hold of her, she started to scream. He got scared that someone would hear her and come to scold him. He didn't intend her any harm, but he throttled her until she was quiet." Ray let out a deep sigh. "He thought she was sleeping."

"So he carried her up to the road?"

"When he couldn't wake her up, he was afraid there was something wrong. He took her to a place where he thought someone would find her."

"And he took her silk hankie," Amber said.

"A memento," Ray assented. Then he looked around at the faces. "But, as God is a witness, Leland didn't mean to hurt Sally. He doesn't have a mean bone in his body."

"Reckon a judge will take that into consideration, Ray," Luke said solemnly. "We still have to bring him in."

"He won't fight, not if I tell him to give himself up." Ray showed a pained expression. "I was hoping that the Frenchman had found Sally, that he really had been the one who killed her. Leland told me what happened, but I wanted to believe he had only caused the girl to pass out.

Like I said, Leland would never purposely do harm to a girl, especially Sally. He was really taken with her.''

Amber fought the sob that rose in her throat, but she could not help herself. Not wanting anyone to watch her cry, she sought the solace of Cully Deeks. Unable to stop the tears of pain and sorrow, she buried her face against his shoulder and wept.

''I think we ought to fetch him in tonight,'' Joe suggested. ''He isn't likely to hurt anyone, but he might get to feeling guilty and run.''

''He wouldn't do that,'' Ray said.

''I'll tell Cole to ready the cell and retrieve the badge I turned in today,'' Luke informed the others. ''Joe, Cully, I'd like you boys to come along.''

''You will only need me,'' Ray told him. ''Leland will do whatever I tell him.''

''I appreciate that, Ray, but we'll do this official like.''

Chapter Twenty-two

Edna placed her hand on Leland's shoulder. He was ashen, both hands on his stomach, but he didn't complain.

"I shouldn't have allowed for you to eat so many of them brownies, son. It's plain you done made yourself sick."

Leland groaned. "It hurts some, Ma."

"Give it a few minutes," she said, patting him on the arm once more. "You'll feel a whole lot better soon. Pepper is right here to keep you company."

In spite of the nausea and chills, Leland slipped a hand out to pat the dog on the head. "Yeah, Ma, he's my dog."

"And a good dog too," she said. "He don't chew the corners of the blankets and he ain't been trying to dig no holes in the floor. He's a good dog."

Leland rolled his head enough to look at Pepper. "Ray says I can teach him to hunt."

"That's fine, son. You two will have a lot of fun together."

The sound of several riders reached Edna's ears. She pulled a blanket up to Leland's shoulders and rose up from his bedside.

"Sounds like your brothers and sister have returned. You rest quiet now."

"Yeah, Ma."

Edna went out the door and closed it behind her. She stood like a sentinel, looking over the group of riders. Ray got down first, his face displaying enough guilt that she knew why the others had come along.

"They figure the Kensington girl couldn't have been killed by that Frenchman, Ma."

"I commenced to think that way too, son."

"This here is Luke Mallory." Ray rotated around to point him out. "The Indian is Joe, and Deeks and Sis are back the road apiece."

"Ma'am," Luke greeted her, touching the brim of his hat. "We're real sorry about this."

"My boy wouldn't hurt no one a'purpose," Edna spoke up for Leland. "What he done were an accident. The girl teased him. He misunderstood is all."

"I believe you."

Donny took a step forward. "They want to take him to jail, Ma. We promised there would be no trouble."

"I'll stay with him in town," Ray offered. "He don't have to face this alone."

Edna held up a hand to block the way. Ray and Donny both stopped in their tracks as the elderly woman stared at Luke. "You acting for the law, are you?" she asked.

"Yes, ma'am."

"Then you best light down. I'll show you to my boy."

Luke dismounted and Joe took the reins of his horse. As he approached the house, Edna rotated around and pushed open the door.

"I 'spect you best wait for the buggy," the woman said. "You'll be needing it to cart Leland into town."

Luke moved enough to look past the woman. He froze in his tracks and gaped. The man on the bed was staring at the ceiling, his eyes wide and glazed. A dog was licking a lifeless hand, as if expecting more attention.

"Ah, no!" Ray exclaimed, rushing past Edna. He pushed the dog aside and dropped onto his knees at the bed. He took hold of Leland's hand, but there was no life left in the body.

"We takes care of our own," Edna stated firmly. "If you want to haul someone before a judge, I reckon it'll be me."

"Why did . . . ? I mean, how . . . ?"

"Wolfsbane in the brownies," Edna explained. "Ray done told me what happened. I knew my boy had kilt that girl. It warn't no fault of his. He never did have a whole deck of cards, but he was a good boy. It was a tragic accident, that's all."

"The judge would have taken that into account, Mrs. Ingersol."

"Leland would have died in prison," she declared. "He would have been ridiculed and called names for being slow. I couldn't allow that."

Luke didn't know what to do, but he didn't intend to arrest Edna for the murder of her son. She had dealt out her own personal form of justice. "I'm sorry" was all he could say.

"We are all sorry," Edna said. "I'm sorry for the girl's folks and I'm sorry for my son."

Luke got back on his horse. Cully and Amber arrived as he was turning for town.

''What's going on?'' Cully asked. ''What about Leland?''

''The case is closed, Deeks,'' Luke told him. ''We're finished here.''

Amber was out of the buggy the moment it stopped. She ran into the house and Cully heard her gasp. He stared at Luke for answers.

''Leland is dead. There's nothing more we can do.''

''Dead?''

''Got hold of some bad food and died. Reckon he has paid the ultimate price for the death of Sally Kensington.''

''What now?''

Luke nudged his horse for town. ''We get on with our lives. As for myself, I left me a pretty girl at the dance, and I'd darn well better get back to escort her home.''

''I expect these people will want some time to be alone,'' Cully said. ''I'll see you boys later. I'm heading back to the ranch.''

''Think there will be any punch or sandwiches left at the dance?'' Joe asked. ''I haven't eaten a bite since morning.''

''Might be if we hurry. We'll kick up some dust on the way back.''

Edna stood in the night air and watched the three men leave. She could hear Amber's sobs and knew the grief Ray and Donny were feeling. She felt in her heart she had done what had to be done, but it didn't make it any easier. If the law demanded a jail sentence for her, she would accept the punishment. Nothing they could do to her would ever equal the pain of what she already felt inside. Leland had always been a good boy. She was going to miss him.